"Kyle Seib~~~~~ ~~~~~~~~~~~~~~~~ ~~d
wild, full of unexpected turns and bizarre images, w~~~~ ~~~~~~~~ght
of that which is deeply and mysteriously human."

—Phil Klay, author of *Redeployment*

"When I read one of Kyle Seibel's stories, I feel like I've met the characters: they are as rounded as they are real, as surprising as they are peculiar. He knows that small interactions are endlessly interesting, and in Kyle's seamless skill, the technicalities of plot, setting and character are considered and elegant. The characters in Kyle's stories are not heroes: some of them are awful; some assholes; some are ravaged by ambition or insecurity; many are hilarious; all believable; all brilliant."

—Pádraig Ó Tuama, host and author of *Poetry Unbound*

"Kyle Seibel has been there, done that, and he writes about it with understated humor, beauty, and lyricism. His stories are provocative and profound, his flawed characters portrayed with nuance and empathy. The result is a book that's massively enjoyable—and deeply indelible."

—Davy Rothbard, author of *My Heart is an Idiot*, creator of *Found Magazine*

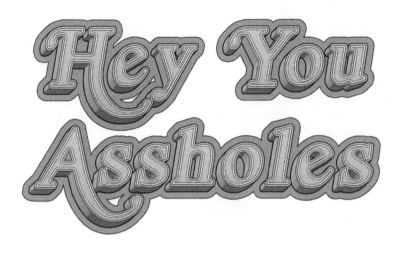

stories by

FICTION

Copyright © 2025 by Kyle Seibel
Cover and typeset by Matthew Revert
ISBN: 9781960988393

CLASH Books
Troy, NY
clashbooks.com
All rights reserved.

For Ali, my everything.

Table of Contents

Part 3

PART ONE

I don't know how to tell you this,
but I'm not really here.

Unfaithful Starring Richard Gere & What's Her Name

The secret truth of working at a movie theater is that you are in charge of protecting the somber catalog of so much human loneliness. Which is why I didn't tell anyone about seeing Bryan and Ron's mom in the audience of Unfaithful, starring Richard Gere and what's her name.

She's the main one. The actress, I mean. It's her movie, really. Richard Gere plays the husband against type. The scene I'm thinking about, the scene where his wife is bathing and she's thinking about this other man, this handsome Spaniard and his wife is oh god what's her name and Richard Gere comes in from work and sees her all steamy in the bath and says to himself why not and takes off his suit and we see his flabby old man body slide into the tub behind Diane Lane, that's her name.

She's an artist. She does something with art. She owns a gallery or a bookstore. And you know, they shot it in Montreal to make it look like New York but it ends up looking like any big dumb city, which I suppose is really the point. She meets a handsome Spanish man who sells old books. She wants to buy them or maybe *she* has some old books and *he* wants to buy them. Either way, Diane Lane and the Spanish antiquarian start an affair. It's pretty horny stuff.

There is a whole other part of this movie that involves Richard Gere killing the handsome Spanish man. He rolls him into a rug and it just becomes this huge other thing. Really derails the final third. I say this of an authority earned during the cumulative ten times I watched it, standing in the back of the theater when I am seventeen and it's my job to stand in the back of the theater wearing a maroon vest and white button down and to make sure the movie looks okay and no one is being an asshole or recording it.

Anyway, Bryan and Ron, they're twins from school and they don't have a dad, just a mom and their mom is young—younger than all the other moms—and she buys a ticket for the Tuesday 7:10, and then again on Wednesday, the 9:40, the last showing, and I tear her ticket and tell her where to go and

I don't think she knows who I am. She doesn't know that I was one of the swim team boys who spent the night before sectionals on her living room floor in a sleeping bag that still smelled like campfire in front of a blinking DVD menu screen for Fight Club. She doesn't know that I was the only one still awake when she got home from wherever she was to check on us before she went to bed and she doesn't know that in the stillness of the room, I could smell on her clothes cigarette smoke lingering with whatever was left of her perfume and she also doesn't know I watched her step carefully around our sleeping bodies to find and kiss both her sons, gently on the head.

Tuesday I couldn't be sure it was her but Wednesday I get a good look. Her movie is the last to let out and she is the last to leave. She walks across the carpeted lobby like a woman who had gotten what she came for and it was worth it.

I'm outside throwing the last of the trash away after locking up and she's still there, leaning against her car, a Kia, smoking. She motions over to me and I point like, Who me? and she laughs because it's an empty parking lot at midnight.

She says, Do I know you from my boys? And I say Yeah, she does. She asks about swim team and I tell her I quit and she asks why and I point to my nametag which reads HEAD

Hey You Assholes

USHER and she nods, exhaling smoke in a narrow stream aimed just to the left of where my head is.

She says, Do you know what I like about that movie? And I say, No, what? And she says, I like how it ends.

Unfaithful starring Richard Gere and Diane Lane ends with the husband turning himself in for the crime of murdering the handsome Spanish man. I ask her what she likes about the end and she looks at me, past me, into the future when this will all make sense and says, Justice.

In a couple years the mall will be gone and then it will be a homeless camp and then it will be a farmer's market and finally it will become what is called an unincorporated non-residential zone and it's about this time, a thousand miles away, that I'll be in the middle of complaining about something at work when I'll see them on the news, Bryan and Ron, in red hats and camo pants, another story in a series of stories about the riot in the Capitol and the people getting arrested.

No names, but it's them. The twins from school in ratty blonde beards and the chyron below their mugshots scrolls past to say they were convinced to turn themselves in by their mother and I have to believe that when they did, it was nighttime and snowing, just like the movie.

Third Shift, Mother Fucker

No more dollies to load the bread trucks.

Corporate says.

New system.

We gotta use these trolleys.

Gotta stack the bread on these little trays.

We stack the trays on the trolleys and roll the trolleys into the trailer. Corporate says to use these straps because now everything's on wheels back there. Moving around and such.

Need a strap for every two rows of stacks and we're putting four stacks in a row. But Corporate only sent two.

Two straps.

Someone says, This is not gonna work.

We're standing around with our dicks up our butts according to the boss. Boss goes, Where's that fucking load you dog fuckers, you lazy dog fuckers. Tell him we need approximately a dozen more straps.

Boss pushes us out of the way.

Big hero.

Puts the only two straps we got on the last two stacks.

Pulls them tight and slaps the side like, Good to go.

Someone says, This is not gonna work.

Driver pulls out the load and goes a little up the ramp.

Straps break or must've because the doors fly open and out come the trolleys. A hundred thousand slices of fresh bread launch into the air and fall all around us.

Swear to god.

Jesus the smell.

Guess who can't believe it.

Boss says he needs to do payroll.

Only four of us there to clean it all up.

This is third shift.

Someone says, I got an idea.

We get a hose.

Wet it all down.

Smash it all together.

Turns into this sludge, this breadsludge.

Roll it into a huge gray ball.

Big as a rhino.

Kinda looks like one.

Heavy too.

Takes half the shift, no shit.

We're covered in the stuff. Slipping in it, even.

It's in our socks, for god's sake.

Someone says, I got an idea.

Gets a forklift from the warehouse.

Puts the wet gray ball of breadsludge in front of the loading dock. Blocks the whole door.

Funny if we left it there, someone says.

Ha ha, someone says.

But then we do.

Leave it there.

Drivers are getting backed up waiting to pick up their loads. Hey what's the deal?

Hey what is that?

We tell them.

They love it.

Everything is delayed.

Ripples out to other shipping centers.

Customers are calling.

Corporate too.

Ha ha, someone says.

Boss yells at the drivers to get off their asses and move the bread. They don't.

Overtime for them no matter what this asshole says.

Boss comes over to us.

Singing a different song now.

Begs us to move it.

Starts crying.

Big hero.

Someone gets the forklift and moves the ball of bread out to the street. We clear the truck line. Boss turns back into an asshole. Surprise, surprise.

Calls us dog fuckers but we know he can't really do shit.

Better chance he'll be the one to get promoted to customer. We clock out, still covered in breadsludge.

Boss is still there when we show up for our shift the next day. Bread's still there too.

Not that it's really bread anymore.

Sun-dried in our time away.

Birds and flies all over it.

Starting to draw attention.

It's not a great neighborhood.

Hey You Assholes

What's the plan there, we say.

Boss says to mind our fucking business.

Anyway, these tweakers come by later and set the dried breadsludge on fire. Tall whooshing flames.

Big ass column of smoke.

The whole deal.

Guess who can't believe it.

Cops start calling.

Corporate too.

Boss starts crying.

Big hero.

We go outside to watch.

Jesus the smell.

Mr. Dubecki's Secret Menu

Mr. Dubecki is the first person I tell about the people humping in the men's restroom because he is the franchise owner slash store manager for one thing, but also because he's the only other person here after Greg went home sick and Rocky's brother picked him up early and the new girl who's training on the window would only get in the way, so she got cut and Mr. Dubecki came by to help me close.

Near the end of the shift I go to clean the facilities and what I find is that it's a four-legs-under-the-stall kind of situation, which I relay back to Mr. Dubecki, who rubs his face like this is the last thing he needs, people humping in the bathroom, oh perfect. I don't think this is the only Taco Bell he owns, but I can see from his face that this was the Taco Bell Mr. Dubecki had hoped people would never hump in.

I follow him into the bathroom and you can basically tell

from the noises that it's two guys and they're not hiding it, not even close. We're both standing outside the stall and I'm waiting for Mr. Dubecki to lay down the law but he doesn't. The panting and grunting is coming from the stall but when I look at Mr. Dubecki his eyes are closed and his head is cocked like he's straining to hear something far away.

I nudge him and he clears his throat real loud but that does not stop the humping. Mr. Dubecki knocks on the stall door. Hello, Mr. Dubecki says. The humping stops.

What do you want, a voice says.

Mr. Dubecki sputters without sound, like his mind is grasping for a response that makes sense and cannot find one. It's like watching someone drown. I jump in and say, We want you to stop humping in this Taco Bell.

This seems to put the world back together for Mr. Dubecki. He follows up by saying, Yes, please leave this Taco Bell. We allow them a moment of silence to consider our demands.

Fine, okay, whatever, says the voice.

We wait outside while they reorder themselves and Mr. Dubecki holds the door open for them. They're two pretty regular looking guys. Mr. Dubecki asks them to please not come back to this Taco Bell.

　　　　　　　　　　　　Hey You Assholes

After we close up, when Mr. Dubecki is locking the doors, he says, Thank you for that back there, and nods in the direction of the bathrooms and I tell him, No problem. He says, You're okay, you know that? When you started, I was eh, not so sure about you. Thought you'd be here through the summer and then go back to school. But hey, you stuck around and I'm happy, really. You're one of the good ones.

He says it like I've cleared some bar with him on a personal level and what comes next is going to be a whole new thing between us.

He says, I have two questions for you. I say, Okay. And he says my first question is this: how would you like to make five hundred dollars and my second question is this: do you believe that stealing something back that was yours first, yours to begin with, that someone stole from you, do you believe that has both a legal and moral justification?

I think about it for a second and then say yes to both.

There are some things, Mr. Dubecki explains, some things in the basement of his house that belonged to him and there had been a situation where now he wasn't allowed back there so much on the order of the future ex-Mrs. Dubecki who was being pretty unreasonable, truth be told. And what he needed, what he really needed, was someone who could keep their cool, just like I did back in the bathroom, just a guy who calls a ball a ball and a strike a strike. Someone who can find a few boxes of stuff the future ex-Mrs. Dubecki would never miss. He says that she hasn't even been in the basement for a year. Do it during the daytime when she'd be at work and the kid would be at school. There's a fake rock with a key in it and he says he can draw me a map, so easy. Five hundred bucks. Mr. Dubecki says that he sure could use five hundred bucks, the divorce and all, but this stuff I'm going to get, it means that much to him.

I think about it for a second and then say, Okay, Mr. Dubecki, and he smiles and says, Please call me George, and I say, Okay, George, and we make a plan for the coming Tuesday.

* * *

On Tuesday I find the key in the fake stone just like Mr. Dubecki said and when I open the door into the house everything is covered with buttery light from the big windows and it's all over the white carpet and all over the white furniture.

Hey You Assholes

I find the basement no problem, find the shelves no problem, find the three boxes no problem. They're pretty heavy so I'm taking them one at a time. I'm on my first trip to the car when I hear a small voice from above say, Hello?

It's the kid. Mr. Dubecki's son. He's standing at the top of the stairs. I say, Hello, and he says, Hello, and I say, I'm one of your dad's special friends. He says, Okay, and I say, I came to get some of his things, and he says, My mom will be back later, and I say, Okay, and he says, Okay.

He looks like a little Mr. Dubecki. Same moon face and turned-up nose. He sits on the top of the stairs and watches me go back and forth. Supervising.

This is my last one, I say, nodding at the box I'm holding, and the kid says, Okay.

I ask him what grade he's in and he says third. He asks me what grade I'm in and I say I'm sort of in college. He asks me what that means and I say, Well, I'm supposed to be in college.

Kind of like how you're supposed to be in school, I say, and he says, Yeah but I got sent home. My mom had to come get me.

Some kind of fight, I say and he shakes his head.

He asks if I've ever heard of a game called Charlie Charlie and I say no and he asks me if I want to play, and I say, Does it take very long, and he smiles and runs off and comes back with two pencils and a piece of paper.

We go to the kitchen and he draws a cross in the center of the paper, making four boxes. In the top two boxes he writes YES and then NO and then on the bottom two boxes he writes NO and then YES so that each quadrant contains a word and is reflected diagonally across from the other. He lays one pencil down along the horizontal line and the other one he balances on top except this one is along the vertical line and he asks me what I want to know.

What do you mean, I say.

You ask Charlie what you want to know, he says. Any question, yes or no.

Who's Charlie? I ask and he says that Charlie is a demon or something and so I think about it for a second and then say, Will I be rich one day?

The kid nods and grabs my hands to make a circle around the piece of paper. He closes his eyes and says, Charlie Charlie, come out to play. We've asked our question, now what do you say? We wait a few seconds and sure enough the

Hey You Assholes

pencil on top, the one balancing, starts to wobble and then swivels to point at both NOs.

Well shit, I say to the kid, and he asks me if I want to know the trick.

He says you do it with your nose. Just blow with your nose really lightly and it's enough to move the pencil but not enough for anyone to notice.

Not bad, I tell him. Why'd you get sent home?

The kid looks away. He says, I asked Charlie if everyone was going to die and then I made Charlie say yes we all would. He looks back at me. Some kids started crying, he says.

Jesus, I say.

But it's true, he says.

I guess, I say. And then, Don't tell your mom I was here.

Don't tell my dad I got in trouble.

We shake on it and I give him a little punch on the shoulder. I tell him, You're okay, you know that, and he shrugs like he doesn't really believe me and it's at that moment when the future ex-Mrs. Dubecki walks in the front door with a few bags of groceries to see a strange man in her kitchen who is touching her son.

* * *

Hello, I say, and she says, What the fuck is happening, who the fuck are you, get the fuck away from him, what the fuck, what the fuck, I'm calling the police right now, you sick bastard.

The kid says, Mom, stop, he's one of dad's special friends, and I say whoa a whole bunch of times in a row while I try to think of what to tell her.

George, I say, stepping back from the kid. George sent me to get some of his things. The basement, the boxes in the basement. The key in the rock. Then I saw the kid. Jesus, please don't call the police.

The future ex-Mrs. Dubecki looks at me, looks at her phone, looks at the oranges that rolled out of the grocery bag she dropped when she saw me, bends down to pick them up, starts crying, slumps over, and then kind of rolls to prop herself up against the wall. The kid goes over to her and says I'm sorry and then I say I'm sorry. And because it would be weird if she didn't, the future ex-Mrs. Dubecki says, I'm sorry. Then we all do it again. Each one of us says sorry again and then I decide to pick up the oranges which breaks the spell.

I put the groceries on the kitchen counter. Mrs. Dubecki watches me. She's standing up now, assessing me. You're pretty young, she says, and I say, I guess so, and she suppresses a sob while saying, Are you happy? I don't know what to say, so I say, I guess so, and she blubbers, Together, with George, you're happy together at least?

Well, I think he's doing okay. It's not like we work together all that much, I say. The future ex-Mrs. Dubecki's face changes. She puts her hands on her hips and she asks me how I know George and I tell her Taco Bell, and she says, Oh, Jesus, I thought you were his—I don't know what they call it—boyfriend, I guess.

Oh, I say.

You didn't know, she says.

No, I say.

Well, she says. Neither did I for a long time.

The kid runs off upstairs. We put the groceries away together, she and I. After, she walks me to the door. I'm not evil, she says. I'm getting my mind around it. Good days and bad days. I mean, there's a version of myself that's happy for him and I'm going to be that woman. Really.

I tell her I think that's a good way to think about it and she asks me if he's doing okay and I think of Mr. Dubecki's face in the bathroom, far away.

Ask Charlie, I say.

* * *

I'm closing that night at Taco Bell and Mr. Dubecki comes by to get the boxes from me. He counts out five one-hundred-dollar bills. He asks me if I had any issues and I say, Not really.

Mr. Dubecki is putting the last box in his car when he stops and asks me if I want to see inside the boxes and I say, Okay. We're standing around the trunk of his Camry in the Taco Bell parking lot and what's inside the boxes is yearbooks and photos and letters and book reports and birthday cards and school newspaper articles and Christmas lists and dental x-rays and baseball cards and bronze baby shoes and souvenir mugs and swim meet ribbons and playbills and bible camp postcards and wrestling trophies and license plates and standardized test scores and watercolor paintings and Mr. Dubecki takes out each item, gives a one-word description, then passes it to me and I look at it and then put it back in the box. It feels like church. We do it for all three boxes and when we're done, Mr. Dubecki steps back to take it all in.

Well, he says finally and grabs a box and starts walking toward the dumpster. C'mon, he says to me, and I grab a box and follow him. I ask him if he wants to maybe just keep the photos and he stares at me. Especially not the photos, he says. We throw it all away.

The purge fills Mr. Dubecki with nervous energy and he bounces alongside me as I walk back towards the Taco Bell to finish my shift. He puts his hand on the door before I can open it.

I'm going to let you in on a little secret, he tells me, and I say, Okay.

His mouth is pressed into a hard line and his eyes are narrowed to make two deep creases in his forehead. There's something called the enchirito, he says. It's not on any menu, but I can teach you how to make one for your shift meal, if you want. It's basically a smothered burrito if you've ever had one of those, but it's really, really good. I keep asking corporate to put it on the menu, but they always ignore me.

Truth is, they're not ready for everyone to experience the enchirito.

Mr. Dubecki's face goes far away. Maybe they're right, he says. He opens the door for me and we go back to the kitchen and he starts gathering the ingredients. Mr. Dubecki's skin is shiny under the fluorescent lights. He looks brand new, fresh out of the packaging.

Okay, he says, tying an apron on. What I'm about to show you is extremely sensitive information.

I watch him run around and I write down the recipe. I tell him his secrets are safe with me.

The Rules of Being a Ghost

I get to work early because it's one of the rules. There are rules to being a ghost in the Navy.

I say rules, but there is really only one—refrain from the remarkable. Some would-be ghosts think the only rule is to be perfect, but being perfect is remarkable, which is against the rules, which means you are not a ghost. Nor does being a ghost mean being a dirtbag. It's a balance.

Take Scroggins, for example. Always late, uniform always fucked up. A second class, but still gets shit from khakis about getting a haircut on a regular basis. Chiefs call him a special case. Bag on him in front of the mess every chance they get. Nickname around the squadron is Petty Officer Cheese Dick.

So Scroggins is definitely not a ghost.

The other example of course is Montoya. One of these recruiting-poster-type guys. Works his ass off for years.

Does everything right. Big gold stars on his service record. Detailer tells him, Hey Joe Navy Montoya, guess what? Because you're so shit hot, you've been selected for special duty in San Diego.

Montoya can't believe it. His whole family lives in San Diego. He tells everyone the good news. Goes on like that for weeks. Except when his official orders come, it turns out he heard it wrong. The special duty wasn't for San Diego. It was for Diego Garcia, which Montoya discovers is a militarized island in the Indian Ocean where he gets involuntarily extended for a total of two years. Or at least it would have been two years if he hadn't killed himself last month.

Anyway. That's why I get to work early. The rules.

I arrive at work one minute before Kaplan, who is another ghost. We are not friends, but we are friendly. Kaplan the friendly ghost, ha ha. We make it a point to arrive before the rest of the shop. No one ever accuses the guys who get there first of not pulling their weight.

Ghosts must do something. It must be something that invites no reward but more importantly, no scrutiny. I am a Safety Coordinator. Meet a girl at the bar and she asks me what I do and I say Safety Coordinator and she says what does that mean? And I take her hand and hold it to my chest and I look deeply into her eyes and I say, It means that I coordinate safety.

But my real job is being a ghost and my real business is accumulating minutes. The long way to the maintenance meeting. Going to another squadron's geedunk just because it's further away. Small talk with the base admin officer. Minutes. When you collect enough, they throw you a big party and send you on your way—with base pay and medical until your last day on the planet.

What I don't tell the girl at the bar is that my principal duty after collecting minutes is watching people pee. My job is to *watch the urine leave the body*. I'm quoting the regulation there. I watch the urine leave the body and into the plastic cup. I stare at the container of urine until it is safely nestled in the cardboard box with the others.

We send the big box of pee to someone else. Who knows what they do with it? They're supposed to test it but I don't care if they store the boxes unopened in a warehouse or whether they pour each one down the sink.

I mention this to Kaplan, that I have no concept of the urine after we send it off. Kaplan says he doesn't either. Says he doesn't think about it at all. Says he can spend all day looking at penises and pee and he'll go home and talk to his wife about the last thing he heard on the radio. And she'll go, Oh really? And on and on and it never comes up.

Outside the shop, lined against the bulkhead, we can hear the shuffling and murmur from our morning crowd of urinators.

Are you ready to serve your country? Kaplan asks me, opening the door.

* * *

By mid-morning we're through most of them when some kid, some new check-in, says he can't go. Tells me like he'd tell a doctor. I tell him to chug some coffee and come back. He shakes his head. Says Chief told him not to return until he'd given his sample. Anyway, he says. He doesn't like coffee. I put him at the empty desk in the corner. Of course he doesn't have any money so I get him a Sprite and tell him he owes me two bucks.

End of the day, he's the last one on my hit list. Says he's got a nervous bladder. Been sitting at the empty desk all damn day.

C'mon man, I say. What's it going to take?

He's looking down at his boots.

Wanna try again?

He shrugs and we march down to the head. Just relax, I tell him. Pretend like I'm not here.

It's not that, he says and starts to say something else when his penis erupts in an open throttle stream of urine.

Finally, I say and he looks back at me with a sad smile.

Back in the shop, he signs his name and I seal the plastic cup. He's watching me package up the big box of pee when he asks me where it all goes and I tell him that I don't really think about it.

What happens if they find something, he asks.

Find something? I say.

Like drugs, he says. Like weed.

Will they? I ask him. He nods his head. They kick you out. You know that.

Fuck me, he whispers. Fuck me, he says over and over again.

Ah, who knows, I say. Who really knows how good these tests are?

Yeah I guess, he says.

He's sitting at the desk with his head in his hands as I pack up for the day. I go to the door holding the giant box of pee and I turn off the lights and I wait for him to get up. He doesn't.

C'mon man, I say. You can't stay here.

You could help me, he says in the dark.

Somewhere below us, the hangar bay doors are closing. They rumble and clang shut.

No one can help you, I say.

You could make a mistake, he says and I hear him crying. You could lose the box. Everyone makes mistakes. I make mistakes, you make mistakes, right?

On the door to the shop is a laminated poster they put up after we got the news about Montoya. *You Make a Difference*, it says. *Life Counts!*

Pull yourself together, I say.

The kid follows me to my car. Please don't send it, he begs. I'll lose everything.

I put the box of pee in the car, close the trunk and spin around. I put my finger in his face. Listen, I say. I don't know how to tell you this, but I'm not really here.

That stops him. He asks me what I'm talking about.

The truth is I'm a ghost, I say.

He's still standing there as I drive away. Shouting at me. So full of blood that it spreads up his neck as he begs for help. How embarrassing. He is so alive! It looks just awful.

Lovebirds

So Senior Reyes, the night shift supervisor. I see him and the new airman walking around the hangar bay. Just talking. Honestly, I thought they were working and I've got my binder with me so I come up behind them and go, hey Senior, can you sign off my qual? He whips around and goes NOT NOW. I'm thinking I might get my ass chewed, but then I see the airman, I think it's Haley, Airman Haley. I look at her and she's all flushed. Now I'm thinking what did I interrupt? I look back at Senior and he puts together what I'm putting together. Changes his tune. SORRY SHIPMATE, he says. WHAT DID YOU WANT?

Nothing, Senior, I tell him. No worries.

C'MON, he says. C'MON, YOU WANT A SIGNATURE?

Yeah, I go. And he takes my qual book. Signs off a couple sections, looks up at me and signs off a couple more sections. THERE YOU GO, he says. Airman Haley slinks away.

I tell him thanks and Senior just stands in front of me. DON'T MENTION IT, he says. TO ANYONE.

* * *

Okay, so Senior Reyes. He takes over the maintenance meeting. Guess who he brings to take notes? Fuckin Airman Haley. They go down the list of which bird is up, who's got budget, whatever. End of the meeting and Senior is walking away and Haley takes the big green logbook and whacks it across his butt. I mean like WHOMP. Senior spins around, sees it's her—starts laughing. I shit you not. We're just watching them, the lovebirds. It couldn't have been more obvious if we walked in on them fucking.

The rest of us don't know what to do.

CMC clears his throat. Kinda sweet you ask me, he says.

I'm looking around like what the fuck? Everyone breaks out after the meeting and I catch up to the CMC.

Kinda sweet? I say. What the fuck?

And he goes, Okay, what's your problem?

Well, I say. It's against the regulations.

CMC goes, Okay, what should I do?

I go, I don't know. I'm not the command master chief.

CMC raises his eyebrows and pokes me in the chest. Okay, let's say you're me, he says. And here's your shipmate, your brother. Married to the Navy. Just about to retire. Now he meets the kind of girl he should've met twenty years ago and that's his fault? Oh, and she likes him too? You're going to tell him to knock it off?

I guess not, I say.

You guess not, CMC says.

Fuck, I say, shaking my head.

My thoughts exactly, CMC says.

* * *

Couple months go by and I start dating the corpsman, right? I'm over at her place and I mention Senior Reyes and she goes, OH MAN. She starts to say something before she stops herself. But now I'm like, You gotta tell me.

She says Haley was part of the maintenance crew that was doing touch and gos on the Vinson a couple of weeks ago and it was Haley's first time on the boat and she thought it was just motion sickness but eventually she went to get a pregnancy test and yep you guessed it.

No shit, I say and she says, Yes shit.

What's gonna happen now? I say.

Well, I think they're gonna keep it, she says.

It? I say.

Her, she says.

Her? I say.

Well, they're hoping, she says.

Hoping? I say.

For a girl, she says.

Back at the squadron, they're not even acting like it's a secret. Haley waits for Senior by his car at the end of the day and they drive off together.

They're gonna make it official and everyone thinks, Good for them. Sure, there's an age gap but consenting adults and all that. One of them will have to transfer. There are protocols to follow. This has happened before. An old story.

* * *

On the news they call it a microburst. An isolated and violent weather event. They say it comes out of nowhere. They say it took the little fishing boat that Senior and Airman Haley were on and sucked them out to sea. It gets a few minutes near the end of the local broadcast. They show Senior's official command photo in his dress blues. For Haley, her driver's license picture.

The funeral makes the front page of the base paper. They invite everyone in the squadron. It's a whole thing.

Day after, I'm sitting in my car outside the flightline before work. Just staring at the dashboard. Someone knocks on my window. It's the CMC. He asks me if I wanna tell him I told him so.

Will it make me feel better? I ask him. Would it have mattered?

Probably not, he says.

What's the lesson here? I ask him.

CMC says, Oh, you wanna learn something? Go to college.

I get out of the car and we're walking together to the turnstiles when WHOMP two birds fly into the briefing room window. We watch them drop to the ground. I start

Hey You Assholes

going over to where they fell and CMC says, What're you doing? but I go over to them anyway. I crouch down and can feel him standing behind me. I'm just trying to figure it out, you know? Tiny crushed beaks and twitchy little feet. I need it to make sense. I'm down there for a while and CMC says, C'mon shipmate. I stand up. We're still looking at the birds when the base 1MC starts playing colors. We turn towards the flag and salute the national anthem and when we look down again I shit you not the birds are gone. They're just gone. And I'm looking at the CMC like what the fuck? and he's just looking at me with this little smile.

Kinda sweet, you ask me, he says.

The Two Women

I am writing this in the car right after it happened because I know how you don't like embellishments, I know that's one of our things, so I'm writing it down because I want to make sure it all comes out like it happened and none of the details get lost, which is another one of our things, and I hope that you see this as growth, as me growing.

I am writing this in the parking lot of the grocery store, the one you like, the one with Jason's fancy turkey, because I'm getting it just for him, I'm making special sandwiches, and I know we talked about gifts, re: overdoing it, etc., but I'm only human, Liz, and they're just sandwiches, albeit, yes, special.

Anyway I am standing in the deli line behind the first woman I'm writing to you about, a woman in an evening gown, one of these wacky ones, and she's asking me about the meat or whatever like I work there and I tell her, Sorry,

I don't work here, and she has this look on her face like she doesn't believe me, like I'm the wacky one, like I'm the one wearing the evening gown to the grocery store on a Thursday afternoon.

This woman says she knows things, says she's a numerologist who has gifts in astrology and that makes her an interpath or exopath or astromorph or ecto something, and she says she knows things about me and honestly, at first, I'm not wild about this interruption because I'm going to be cutting it close picking up Jason and being late is one of our things and I hope you can tell that lately I've really been trying.

But this woman says, You've recently learned someone's secret, and then reaches out and grabs my shoulder and she says, You're a Gemini and you've recently learned someone's secret and you're going through a lot right now and I can help you, and she gives me a little squeeze with each of those last words so it feels like this: I (squeeze) can (squeeze) help (squeeze) you (long squeeze).

What I haven't told you is what I found when reviewing footage from my security camera and what I also haven't told you is that I recently installed a security camera to figure out what is going on with my packages, about how I find them delivered at my door, opened but no items missing, opened but just messed with, somehow.

And what I haven't told anyone and probably never will outside these words to you is that I saw the old man who lives down the hall come by my door while I was at work and open a package and take out the air-filled plastic bags they use as fillers and put them under his shirt and arrange them like breasts and rub them very tenderly and return them to the box and then clap his hands like, That's done, and walk away.

I'm looking at the lady in the evening gown and suddenly she doesn't look so crazy because as it turns out I am a Gemini, I have recently learned someone's secret, and I am going through a lot right now and so if those things are true, could the other thing also be true, re: helping me, etc.?

The next thing she says is that Barack Obama is a homosexual and Michelle Obama is also a homosexual and do I know what adrenachrome is (I don't) and would I like to find out (I would not) and my brain is buzzing because I'm starting to feel like the rest of my life, the life I'm living without you, will be a series of events that make less and less sense until I will be completely untethered from the planet.

Hey You Assholes

The concept of it swallows me, a black hole of a thought, and that's why I don't notice at first when the other woman approaches me, the other woman I'm writing to you about, the older Hispanic woman who comes up behind me while I'm loading in groceries and touches my elbow and who, when I turn around, motions for me to follow her across the street and softly says, You help me.

It's like I don't even have a choice because I follow her to an apartment complex where we walk up three flights of stairs to a room where all the lights are turned off and where there are two suitcases sitting by the door and the woman points to the bigger of the two and then back out to the street and says, You help me.

I pick up the bigger suitcase and follow her down the stairs and we walk half a block to the bus stop and that's where she motions for me to put the suitcase and then motions for me to bend down and then motions for me to get closer, which I do, which is when she kisses my cheek like the pope and says, You help me.

Between helping the second woman and writing it all down, I know I'm going to be late picking up Jason, but Liz, I feel very strongly about telling you this and what I'm trying to say is that whatever else I've done, the person who this happened to is the truest version of who I am, and I have to think there's some cosmic purpose to it, that you can draw conclusions here, that it balances out, the two women, the old man, the suitcases, the evening gown, that it's evidence of a universe which seeks harmony with itself, a universe where, please goddamnit, one day, I can come home and for that to mean a place with you and Jason but especially and only you, I promise, this time, forever.

Dirty Lincoln

This one's called Dirty Lincoln and it's for waiters and such. Okay, so you're doing your job, doing your job, la la la, and the family of dorks in your section finishes their plates of slop. They pay in cash and their change is, let's say, eight bucks. Three ones and a five. Now, you want a tip, deserve a tip, and you want the five, not the three, and ideally you want the whole eight. So you take the five and you really fuck it up. Working at a Thai place in Tampa and the guy who showed me this would use syrup from the soda gun to make it sticky because no one wants sticky money so nine times out of ten, the dad dork tips the five and most of the time, the whole eight. Dirty Lincoln.

* * *

I got the job at the Thai place through a friend of the woman I was living with, a woman who believed I was transitioning out of the Amish community. She believed this because that's what I told her the night we met at Tiny Taps.

Drinking on a stool and she came up next to me to order at the bar. Big dangly earrings and one of those skirts, I don't know what you call it. Short. She caught me looking over at her so I shot my eyes away. Saw an Amstel Light bottle and I think Amstel Amstel Amtrak Amber Ambush Amish Amish Amish Amish.

"Sorry for staring," I said, getting her attention. I patted my chest. "Amish," I said. "For what it's worth, I'm Amish."

"You don't look Amish," she said.

I took a deep sigh. "I did until very recently."

"Where's your beard?"

"Shaved it," I said, hanging my head. "I'm starting all over."

She smiled. "Me too."

After three bourbons for me and two whiskey sours for her she said, "Can I tell you something crazy?" and I pretended to really think about it before I said okay, like I'm still catching on to the way this wild world works.

She said, "I had a dream about this and I think you're supposed to come live with me and I think we're supposed to get married," and in response, I squared my shoulders and looked unblinking into her round and brown little face and I, with the voice of some asshole who had built barns until he just couldn't anymore, said, "Sweet sister, we had the same dream."

* * *

Always feels longer when I tell it, like it was years together in that basement studio with the girl from the bar who ended up being named Saritza, but I was only there for a couple weeks because I'm only anywhere for a couple of weeks, or at least that's how I was then.

Fun at first. Punching buttons on the microwave all confused. Getting overwhelmed in the headphones aisle at Best Buy. That kind of thing. And you know, she never suspected I was anything other than what I told her, even though she would have understood at some point that wonder wears off. I kept doing it though. I kept doing it because I couldn't stop. I was addicted.

Each time I faked a culture shock panic attack, she would comfort me, but not how you're thinking. The girl had a gift. She pulsed out electrosympathetic neurowaves of pure human soul that transformed her face into a Valentine's Day heart and her pupils would swell and crystal tears dripped off long lashes and she would take me in her arms or crawl into my lap and she'd squeeze what she thought was the sad out of me and I would squeeze her right back and we would cry and fuck each other's brains out because she was starting over too, starting over for real, and she must have thought I never asked about it because I was too green to understand what she was running from, but really, I just didn't give a shit. The only shits I gave were for those times between us when I was wrapped inside her and she'd smush me until the black parts of my eyes spread to the edges of my face.

Until, of course, like all drugs, it stopped working.

* * *

Long shift at the Thai place and I'm beat up afterward because honest work is bullshit and all I want is my sweet Saritza to pour out into me with her fiery little person except

Hey You Assholes

I'm also too gassed to think of something I hadn't marveled over yet.

We were looking for something to watch when I muttered, "So many movies." Except I say it all dreamy, like I'm talking about something deeper than HBO but Saritza was on her phone at the other end of the couch and not really paying attention. Frankly, she had been cooling on my shit since the previous Sunday when I got drunk and told her one pretty friend that she had skin like churned butter.

"What," Saritza said.

I pointed to the TV and made a face like I'm just so lost and eventually we whipped it up into something that resembled our sessions from those first days. She did her thing and we cried and fucked but it wasn't any good and that's when I started thinking, not for the first time, that I have to get out of this miserable goddamn state.

* * *

I'll never know how she found out but gun to my head, I'd bet it was her friend that I hit on. Also, I ordered a few boxes of bulk SIM cards on the internet, another story, and had them delivered to the apartment which, looking back, was not my smartest move. Saritza pressed me about it one morning over coffee. I mean, she went right for it.

"You're not Amish," she said. Her knees were pulled up to her chest, tucked inside the old shirt she slept in.

I blinked a few times. "I know baby, not anymore. You're helping me so much."

She stared at me, jaw muscles jumping. "No, you've never been Amish."

I looked up, away from her gaze. "Mennonite, then."

"No," she said.

I looked back at her then and saw in her eyes the unmistakable wound of new wisdom. This was the end. "No," I said, agreeing with her. "I've never been Amish."

She nodded and swallowed and put her face down through the neck of her t-shirt and screamed. When she was done, she looked at me and said, "I think there's something wrong with you."

"You could say that about anyone," I replied, which ended up being the last thing I ever said to her. We sat there for a while, but she was still crying when I got up to pack my things. I felt about a hundred years old.

Hey You Assholes

Called the Thai place to see if I could pick up a shift on my way out of town and the guy who taught me Dirty Lincoln made it happen. Thieves' code, I guess. Fucked up the drawer for who- ever was closing that night but made off with a couple hundred bucks from the lunch crowd. Enough for a bus to nowhere fancy which in this case meant Hattiesburg, Mississippi.

The Greyhound station in Hattiesburg is next to a Cracker Barrel, which I ate at, which tasted like dust, like nothing at all, and I walked the half mile down Route 49 to the Wyndham, where I checked in using a credit card I kept for emergencies, or rather, a credit card someone else kept for emergencies, or did until I took it off them.

The lady at the desk gave me a key card, room 507, and when I swiped it, it didn't work. Went back down and the lady at the desk gave me another one. Go back up, try it again, no luck. Back at the desk. Lady very apologetic.

"What kind of place are you running here?" I demanded.

"I'm very sorry, sir." She did not sound very sorry. She sounded very tired. She clacked some more keys on her computer and handed me another card. "This one should work. I figured out what was wrong, just a little glitch, and now it's just fine, sir. This will work."

It didn't. I threw the card down the hallway. It flicked against the wall. I stomped my way to the elevators, punched the down button, punch punch punch. Down down down. I got in the elevator and when the mirrored doors closed, I screamed goddamnit at myself.

I just wanted to get in the room. I just wanted to be in the goddamn room. I just wanted to be held and stroked and I wanted those tears on me, because her tears were so real and mine were such bullshit. She ruined me for anything else a woman could ever give me. I was her Dirty Lincoln but she didn't want me and neither did anyone else and I would go looking everywhere and never find her again.

The elevator doors opened in the lobby. The lady at the desk looked up from across the room. I could see the apology forming in her neck, but she wasn't sorry, not really. Not yet.

A Couple Jokes About Meat

I am watching my ex-girlfriend's new husband do stand up comedy and honestly it's not bad. It's not bad for a video on the internet, I mean. I found it a week ago but I saved it for right now, for when my current girlfriend is sleeping upstairs because I have played out the scenario of explaining this whole thing to her and I'd just as soon not.

What's this, she'd say. And I'd tell her. And she would say, Oh and in that sound would be the first sentence in a story that ends with her leaving. It would happen even though I'd tell her it's not what she's thinking and she'd say, Okay so what am I thinking.

So I am watching it alone.

Someone shot it on their phone from the first row, so all I see is him. He's short, but then again, she is too. He does a whole section about my ex-girlfriend except, you know, he doesn't call her that. Every joke is a joke about how pathetically in love they are. He says that when they met she told him she was from Wisconsin and he said, Let's go. He said, Let's go to Wisconsin because I want to beat up everyone who was ever mean to you. It gets some laughs and I think, Why didn't I say that?

They're young to be married, first of their friends to get married and now he is riffing on their courthouse wedding. A courthouse! We used to babysit her nephew and we'd push him around in a million dollar stroller and right before we'd get to the park she'd whisper, Let's pretend he's ours and that is the same girl who got married in a courthouse to a comedian. Except he's not just a comedian, I discover. He's also a butcher. A butcher! He does a couple jokes about meat and I think, Why didn't I do that?

We gotta talk about this guy she used to date, he says. The most boring guy in the world.

In the 1950s in Erie Pennsylvania a newspaper interviewed my father. He was six. I don't know why. The clipping used to be pressed in a book on a shelf in a house in Arizona but when my father died it went in a box and arrived six months after the funeral on my front step and inside was all this shit and tucked somewhere was a yellow piece of newsprint and on it was an interview with my father, little Bobby, a first grader, whose bike is broken and who sent a girl in his class three valentines even though she didn't send him one.

Imagine carrying that with you, holding the story in your hands like a perfect apple and sharing it with your girlfriend late at night in hushed tones walking home after the bars close. So when this guy makes some joke about how his wife's ex-boyfriend wasn't very interesting, it's like, okay. That can't be me. It's someone else. The guy she went out with before me, maybe. Or maybe if there was a guy between this guy and me.

Whoever it's about, it's far and away his best stuff. The first true blue guffaws of his set.

This guy, he says, oh man this guy. This guy, he says over the laughter, he was so boring that he just disappeared one day from her mind. Poof, like that. They didn't even break up, didn't even have to, she just erased him, can you believe it.

Yes, I say to my computer. I can believe that.

This guy, he says, this guy was like a ghost in a movie who doesn't know he's a ghost. Know what I mean?

Yes, I say. It's only eight minutes or so but I'm watching it on a loop and I'm on my seventh or so time through when I break a wine glass and shout, Goddamnit which wakes up my current girlfriend and soon I can hear her coming down the stairs. I can feel her walk up behind me but I'm not ready for whatever we have to talk about, not yet, so I don't turn around but instead I restart the video. Pretty soon she's going to ask me what I'm doing and I'm not going to have a good answer. I can hear her lips part and the muscles in her throat flex. Any second now. Here it comes.

Hey You Assholes

The Former Mayor of Baghdad

The former mayor of Baghdad opens a restaurant in my east
Denver neighborhood. He's our guy. Or used to be. He's
the one we installed after we took over. Listen to me. We. I
mean the government. I didn't do shit.

Out there on the sidewalk is how I meet him. He's supervising a new sign being hung out front and I'm, well. Who
knows. Walking, I guess. Since Jenn left I've been having
difficulty connecting to the why of what I'm doing. Find
myself in the grocery store, staring at the shelves. Someone
comes up and goes, Sir, what are you looking for? And
then there's me standing in the aisle with an empty cart,
not knowing what to say. Upsetting when it happens a few
times in a row.

The team working to hang the sign in front of the restaurant takes up the whole sidewalk. Excuse me, I say to the

former mayor of Baghdad, though I won't know that detail until later.

Ah yes, he responds. He holds up one finger. He waves at his crew to pause. He ushers me through. We open next week, he says, giving me his card. Do you like Iraqi food?

I haven't had Iraqi food, I tell him.

This makes him very excited. My friend, he says. Do you know what it will be like? Amazing grace. Yes? You are blind, but you will see.

I tell him maybe. I'm being friendly because that's just how we are in this neighborhood. I'm being friendly because I don't know how to tell him he's doomed. It's a good place to live but he's chosen a bad location for a business. Since I've lived here it's been a brunch spot, a furniture showroom, a design agency, and now it's Al-Basha, Denver's first and only Iraqi restaurant.

I know that because later the same day I find a business journal article about it online. I look it up reflexively. As a matter of course. That's the kind of person I am now, I guess. The kind of person who reads business journal articles online. It's there I discover that the man who owns the restaurant is also the former mayor of Baghdad.

I wonder what the location will be next. After all, it's just a matter of time. The city will reclaim the spot from the former mayor of Baghdad like it did from all the other business owners. His mistake is thinking that he is special. That he is exempt from the rules of nature. He, of course, is not because, of course, no one is.

Listen to me. Like I've got all the answers.

* * *

I'm not the first person in the world to get divorced. It just feels that way. People have been saying to me that it's okay to be sad about this, but when I do, the feeling of despair is too delicious and I can feel the ground shift beneath me as I sink further into the folds of endless gray blankets. So easy to be sad about Jenn, but also sad about everything. So easy to empty all effort into this one comfy dumpster of being miserable all the fucking time.

Yikes, I think.

The important thing is to stay busy. Which wouldn't be so hard except I'm not working right now. I can't explain it any better than this: I woke up one day and was not able to deal with the fact that it was September again.

Jim, I'm sick, I emailed my boss from my phone as I watched all my neighbors climb into their cars from my bedroom window. I had wrapped the bed sheet around me like a wedding dress. *I'm not coming in*, I typed.

That was two weeks ago. I have not replied to subsequent emails which were sent in the guise of checking up on me.

Today I detect a note of panic. *Are you ever coming back??* he asks. Double question marks like it's me making the decisions. He's clueless. I don't respond.

They'll eventually stop paying me. I know that. I just don't give a shit.

* * *

It is too early in the evening to be so drunk except that I am. I am drunk from the bladder of wine I snuck into a big dumb superhero movie that I half-watched, half-slept through.

I'm missing pieces, I say to the Uber driver on my way home. Or like I have them, but they're in the wrong spot. Or like there are parts leftover from assembly still rattling around inside me.

Hey You Assholes

Where do you feel them rattle? The driver has presented himself at the onset of our journey as something of a mystic.

I move around in the backseat, trying to see where I can feel my leftover pieces. Somewhere in my balls, I say.

Interesting, he says. May I ask how much time you spend contemplating God? For me, I would estimate forty percent.

Same, I say.

Let's change the subject, he says. What's your favorite documentary?

I pretend to think about it and then I pretend to fall asleep.

You're home, he says when we arrive at my place.

Eh, I say.

* * *

For the same reason I couldn't handle it being September, I cannot yet face my empty little house. This is how my walks begin and walking makes me recall the former mayor of Baghdad and recalling the former mayor of Baghdad puts me on a trajectory to his doomed restaurant and upon opening the door to Al-Basha, I am greeted with a sweet and warm wall of scents. Beyond it I find a dozen golden blanketed tables, each one stacked with plates and people and towers of food with exotic smelling sauces and wordless, happy noise droning from each chewing face. Music—from the old world, I presume—plinks away in the background.

I shake my head. They have no idea.

There is no room for me among the diners, but there is room for me among the drinkers. I sit at the bar, wave away the menu, and ask for a bottle of their cheapest red wine, which turns out to be a metallic tasting merlot. Listen to me. Suddenly so discerning. Who am I, my ex-wife? I laugh. It occurs to me that's the first time I've thought of Jenn like that.

I mean, in that way. I mean, in those terms.

In response, I drink two glasses fast which leads to me being drunk enough to become master of the universe, an achievement you can unlock with a certain volume and velocity of red wine.

The entire universe now safely under my control, I begin conducting the orchestra of the restaurant around me, telekinetically guiding the waitstaff through negotiations with the kitchen and the customers and each other. There is a wild harmony to a room full of smells and people and they should be grateful I am at the helm, that I am drunk enough to ascend to this spiritual plane where I can assign each atom its rightful position in space.

I'll see him now, I say to the bartender after I finish the bottle of wine.

Who? she says.

The former mayor of Baghdad, I say. The owner. We met last week. I have a very important message for him.

The bartender tells me the owner isn't there tonight, but that I can leave my message with her.

Good because the message is this, I say. The message is that you are doomed. That doom awaits you. But not to worry because when you fail it won't be your fault. And the world is simply recorrecting. And you did your best. But it's okay. And even though I didn't try the food, it really seems like some people like it a lot. But also you're still doomed.

I ask the bartender if she wants to write any of this down. She says she has a good memory. I say if you have such a good memory then what was this place before it was Al-Basha?

She says that this place *isn't* Al-Basha, that it's Arnoldi's, that it's been at this location for 15 years. That it's an *institution* in this neighborhood. She looks a little concerned. She says that Al-Basha is the new Middle Eastern place across the street.

Across the street? I say and she hands me my bill.

You're not where you think you are, the bartender informs me.

* * *

There's no bar in Al-Basha. Just a few red tables that would be entirely empty if not for the quiet family of four eating in the corner with their heads bowed. There is no music, no art on the walls, no color at all. Nothing but the untucked maroon shirt of one teenaged waiter. He doesn't move a muscle when I walk in. His face is hidden by hair as he stares at his phone.

I stand there for a little while and I'm about to leave when the former mayor of Baghdad comes out of the kitchen and rushes to meet me at the door. My friend, he says. I knew you would come.

I am unable to tell whether he recognizes me from the sidewalk or whether this is just his schtick. Walking across the street has greatly diminished my powers as the master of the universe. There is no harmony in this place to bend into tunefulness, no energy force to swirl in invisible currents. A sour taste in my mouth replaces my fading winebuzz.

You will have the lamb, the former mayor of Baghdad says. The *quzi*. No argument. Please.

He seats me at the center table—a place of high honor, I assume—and I nod to the quiet family eating in the corner. I am served a plate of yellow rice and blackened knobs of meat. I have a couple bites. It's fine. In some ways, it'd be better if the food was a disaster because then it could be more easily explained to him when forces of nature come for their due. Probably no one has shown him the situation in such clear terms, how it doesn't matter what you do, how hard you try, some things are just black holes. They just take from you, they suck you dry, and even though you can't stop it, it's better to know so you're not so hard on yourself when it all comes crashing down.

My friend, the former mayor of Baghdad says as he takes the seat across from me. He pours a milky liquid from a metal tumbler over ice in two small glasses.

Arak, he says.

I cheers him. *Arak*, I say and drink.

No, he says. This drink is called *arak*.

I cheers him again. *Arak*! I say and drink again.

No, no my friend. This is the name of it. The name. *Arak*.

I thought you were from *arak*? I say.

He pauses. I am from *Iraq*, he says slowly and then catches on and smiles.

I smile back sadly. This poor bastard.

You love the lamb, he says, pointing to my plate.

I wish it were that simple, I say. I finish my *arak*. The former mayor of Baghdad refills my glass. I've come to let you know something, I say. My powers as master of the universe are tingling back into my limbs and I decide to start from a high level.

You are going to die, I say, gesturing with my hand as if to say far ahead, sometime in the future.

The former mayor of Baghdad nods. Yes, he says.

But it comes faster for some men, doesn't it?

Yes, he says solemnly and sips his *arak*.

Like some places, I say. Some places are prone to catastrophe.

Hey You Assholes

I know this, he says.

I shake my head. No, I say. I'm talking about this place, this restaurant. It's something about this spot.

He nods again. Yes, he says. There is something special here.

I bang my fist on the table. No! Goddamnit. You're not listening. You're doomed. Don't you see? It's nothing you did. It's a curse. It's a law of nature.

He bangs his fist on the table back at me. Ahh! he says. See? I can do that too. Hm? Nothing I did? There is no knowing what I have done. Hm? Maybe you are cursed. Maybe you are doomed. Have you thought about that? You think this was my number one choice of the world? You think I had so many choices? Eh? What other spot do they have for me? No spot.

The former mayor of Baghdad drains his glass. I was hunched forward, hands on the table, but now I slump back.

So you know? I say.

Of course I know, he says. I am a businessman.

The man in the family of four signs the check for their meal. I'm trying to nod at him like when I arrived but he won't look at me. I realize he's uncomfortable on my behalf. I am suddenly very sober.

It seemed bigger inside me somehow, I say to the former mayor of Baghdad. It seemed very important to tell you.

Maybe important for *you*, the former mayor of Baghdad points to me and then to himself. But not for me.

The teenage waiter buses my partially eaten lamb. Would you believe I thought I was helping? I ask.

Of course I believe you, he says, splitting the last of the *arak* between our two glasses. American helping. I know this story.

* * *

I know I should wait for the morning to reply to my boss, but I don't. There is a lingering sensation of having learned something and I want to capture it because doing so will mean that it's definable, which means it's fixable, which means someone can finally help me, that I'll finally know how to ask, that if only I could be genuine and honest for once, in this one email, the world's axis would shift back into place and I'm so, so close except for the fact that everything I write is such awful dogshit.

Jim, I write. *For thousands of years, men have suffered.* New paragraph. *I am such a man.*

I replace *men* with *people*. I cross out *such a man* and write *no different*. It's been two hours. I hope I'm not actually going insane. That would be humiliating.

It takes me the rest of the night but I do it. Listen to me. Some kind of grad student.

Listen to me. I mean, please. Anybody. I need someone to know this.

Jim, I write. *I'm starting to feel a little better.*

Fish Man

The children who are helping call me Fish Man. I say helping because they mean well but are mostly in the way. I say children but they're boys, a whole gang of them.

They call me Fish Man because the only thing they know about me is that I am knee-deep in this pond that is quickly draining and I am trying to save the fish. The pond is in the woods behind the school which is how they found me. I say the woods, but you can see it from the road. You can see straight through to the other side where there is a bar in a shopping center which is where I was until a few hours ago.

Sure, I was drinking but that was before I was Fish Man and how it happened was the bartender asked me in no uncertain terms to leave the bar. I say the bar but it's a bar and grill and by that okay, I mean it's a restaurant. *Walk it off, buddy* was the advice I got and I did just that. Walked across the road to piss in the woods and holy shit there's a bunch of fish in those little ponds.

Except they're not little ponds, I discover, taking a closer look. It's a half drained lake.

Some parts are so shallow that the fish are flopping around in the mud. I venture down and nudge one with my foot back into a deeper section.

There you go little guy, I say to the fish. I look down into the pool of water. They look like a hundred green puppies wagging their tails at me.

I take off my shoes and socks and roll up my jeans. I make a pouch with the front of my shirt and start transporting the flopping fish from the shallows to the deeper parts.

That's gotta feel good, I say after dumping a shirt full into the water.

It's then that the group of boys from school arrive and ask me what I'm doing. I don't look up because the fish are slick with mud and scum and it takes all my focus to pinch them by their little fins.

I'm saving the fish, I say. I say it like someone hired me to do it, like I went to school for it.

They goof around watching for a little but eventually take off their shoes and socks too. They mimic my careful movements.

Is it your recess or something, I say.

They say it's the last day of school. They were supposed to go to Six Flags but it got canceled because of the weather.

What's wrong with the weather? I ask.

The boys shrug.

They're doing their best, but they don't have a knack for it. Not like me. I have never been more skilled at any activity than I am at saving these fish. It's a good thing too because in the time that we've been at it, the water level has fallen. At first I think I'm just imagining it, but the boys notice too.

Fish Man, they say, pointing at the stones that were submerged just an hour ago.

I see it, goddamnit.

We tear the sleeves off our t-shirts and wear them like headbands. I feel the cords of my back muscles tighten into a spiral. I grimace and continue. The noble side in an ancient fight. I instruct the boys to go faster.

Yes, Fish Man, they respond in unison.

I make a supply run to the grocery store down the block and return with protein bars and energy drinks. We sit on rock perches and I pass out the rations.

Fish Man, what happened here? the boys ask me.

I take a big bite of protein bar and chew. It used to be a lake but now it's all fucked up, I say.

Why Fish Man?

I gesture out across the mud. Our only job is to save the fish, I say.

The boys nod.

All our work comes down to the final pool. The lake's last stand. The only spot that seems to be holding water. It's teeming with fish. They're jumping all over each other. They look pissed as hell. It's not a perfect solution, but it'll have to do for now. There are no easy decisions left to make.

My life is serious now that I am Fish Man.

The sun is going down. My team needs to get home. Here's what's going to happen, I tell the boys. I've got a truck. I've got a friend who has these giant tanks. Huge ones. And I'm gonna borrow them and we're going to put the fish in the tanks. We'll take them to a bigger lake somewhere else. I pause to look each one of them in the eye. We're going to save them, I say.

The boys high five. I make them promise to meet me here tomorrow.

Thank you, Fish Man. Yes, Fish Man…

Tomorrow we'll return to find the pool of water still holding, but with nothing in it. At some point during the night, each fish will have jumped out to die gasping on the dry lakebed. Gray fish bodies will circle the small pool in the cracked mud. We'll squish around in silence, checking for signs of life and not find any.

Fish Man, what happened here?

I guess they died, I'll say.

Fish Man, why?

You must've squeezed them too hard, I'll hear myself say.

What does that mean?

I'll make a sound like it's obvious, even though I know it isn't.

You're a pervert, one of the boys will say.

A fish pervert, another boy will say.

I'll call them little assholes and they'll all run off. I'll go back to where I parked to find my keys locked in my truck. Phone too. I won't get the job I'm waiting to hear back about. Not the next one either. In fact, I won't get any job ever again. I never make a comeback. I never turn things around. I never understand what happened to those fish…

But that night on the street, standing across from the restaurant that kicked me out just a few hours earlier, I am still under the impression that it's all a good omen. Confirmation that I was born with gifts and purpose. Made for something almost holy.

The streetlights come on. The boys get on their bikes and ride away. I stand there waving in the dark. Troops dismissed. A day's work done. I am filthy, but I am useful. I am Fish Man.

PART TWO

The same asshole making the same mistake.

I Suppose You'll Want to Know Something About my Life Now

Leila died last week, that's the big update around here. We knew it was coming, but it was still hard when we heard it.

I went for a jog right after we got the call, which is something I never do. Abbie had to ask me twice where I was going.

I was down along the beach, that multi-use path parallel to Cabrillo, because I thought it would be nice to watch the waves crash, you know? I was looking for something that could plug me back into the universe, if that makes any sense. The truth is I wasn't really jogging per se. It was more like a shuffle.

I'm not, if you must know, in great shape.

And yes, I was making sure to not bump into anyone or step in any dogshit, but I was *elsewhere*.

You know how I get. My own little world.

Of course I was thinking about Leila. This one time specifically. She had come to stay with us during the summer when we were kids. Dad got tickets to the ball game and even back then—25 years ago at least—she wasn't so good on her feet and our seats were way up there and this was before they built the new stadium with the escalators, so all we could do was walk the ramps, one step at a time, to the upper deck.

A thirteen-year-old me hung back and walked with Leila. I held her hand. She was unsteady on the incline. I needed to hold her hand, yes, but I also *wanted* to. That's what I was thinking of, shuffling along the path. I was remembering the wanting-to.

A white shape in my right peripheral became a large car, a cream-colored SUV, rolling through the crosswalk at Bath Street and coming one centimeter away from smashing right into me. I mean seriously. The closest call I've ever had. You could smell the tire skid. My leg hair was touching the bumper for god's sake.

The end of me, I'm sure of it. Or very nearly, anyway.

The fucking nerve.

In the space of a nanosecond, I went from walking hand-in-hand with Leila to screaming in the face of the driver of the car who almost killed me. I had that high-chested hollow tingly feeling of too much adrenaline and I knew that people were stopping to stare at the lunatic in red running shorts yelling his head off, but I simply couldn't help myself.

I was, I think, unloading something that couldn't be carried any longer.

And this driver, this woman—huge sunglasses, that's all I remember about her face, these gigantic plastic goggles—she didn't even flinch. She was smiling, in fact. She put the car in park. I was still shouting, mind you, though the intensity had waned somewhat. And yes, there was some other emotion mixing in beyond pure rage at this point. I was crying, to say it honestly, which is another thing I never do, which is probably part of the reason why it felt so strange and yes, admittedly, even a little good.

To me, I spent a week screaming at that women, accusing her of attempted murder, standing on that corner near the restaurant I always forget the name of—Chad's? Conrad's?—but it was likely only a minute or so.

The lights changed and the woman drove away and the flood of adrenaline receded. I was suddenly freezing. Eighty degrees, not a cloud in the sky and my teeth were chattering. I sat on the curb and wiped my face with my shirt. I tried to stop shaking but couldn't. Something else too. Something I had even less control over. Between my legs a wild erection had sprung. The Washington Monument, no kidding. A pole of blue steel soldered onto the front of me.

There was no hiding it. Not in those shorts.

I was a mile away from where I parked. A mile at least. My thinking was that moving around may help redistribute the bloodsurge, but really I had no choice. I stood up. My penis bobbed ahead of me. I shuffled behind it on our way back to the car.

Made it halfway before the police officer stopped me.

He wanted to know what the hell I was doing. And had I seen all the families and children out today? And did I think it was acceptable to run around like I was? A grown man in a state of extreme arousal—is that what I wanted kids to see when going to the beach on the weekend? He was doing his best to look me straight in the eye to communicate that he really meant business, but his gaze kept returning to my crotch.

Stop looking at it then, I wanted to say, though I was hardly in a position to issue any demands. He was angry and embarrassed and how could I blame him? He just didn't see the whole situation.

My grandma, I said, gesturing to the boner by way of explaining. I had one last grandma and she died today.

Abbie has since referred to this as my getting-arrested, which is more than misleading—patently untrue, I'd term it—because the only thing that happened is he took me half a mile down the road in the back seat of his squad car to where I'd parked the RAV4 and before he let me out, he told me to take care of myself and to go straight home and you know what? I almost did. I had my keys in the ignition and was about to turn it over when I saw the balloon, which is really what this whole thing is all about.

Just this regular mylar balloon. It had escaped a group of them tied to a picnic table for someone's birthday party. Taking its time disappearing into oblivion. Lingering in the wind. Reminded me of you, weirdly enough. Except not you exactly.

It was this thing Brooke put together the week after they found your body. The official funeral was a small ceremony, private and exclusive to the family. Your uncle covered all the costs, to hear Brooke tell it. This other thing was more like a memorial.

Neptune Beach at sunrise. Mostly people from your office and the Jax Beach bar crowd. You can probably guess who.

Everyone was given a balloon. We went around in a circle and each person said something nice about you. Then they let go of their balloon. I don't think they let you do that now because it's basically littering, but this was ten or so years ago and we didn't care anyway.

Brooke said you had a generous spirit. Mandy said your laugh was a miracle. Other people said other nice things. Everyone was laughing and crying.

When you went missing, I kept thinking I'd be a suspect or a person of interest. I was waiting for the call, but none came. I was almost offended to not be considered. Okay, I was *definitely* offended. I think it made me realize that the time we had together accounted for such a small part of the total person you were. And how that's true for so many other people in my life as well. And how I'm not sure what to do about it.

On my turn, I fumbled around and said something about your inextinguishable joy, which was stupid because that's precisely why we were there—the extinguishing of your joy. I let go of my balloon and followed it among the crowd of the others and even after all theirs had become dots against the clouds, mine stayed at a lower altitude, stuck in the coastal wind churn and I stayed too, watching it after everyone was long gone.

Now, I know it doesn't mean anything. I know it wasn't you telling me you're in heaven or whatever. I'm not saying that. All I'm saying is seeing the balloon down by the beach like that after the SUV and thinking about Leila—well, it *reminded* me. And it felt nice even though it was also pretty sad, which is a thing that's been happening to me more often.

Leila died last week. That's when all the SUV and balloon and boner stuff happened. We're still in the after-shocks. Shows up in unexpected places. Abbie opened the door to the fridge to load in some groceries the other day and started crying. Oh, what's the point, she said and went off upstairs.

Things like that.

Things like this, too. Sitting at the kitchen table. Drinking too much. Thinking too much. Writing these little letters to you in the middle of the night.

It's been suggested, by Abbie herself no less, that what I am is still in love with you. But I firmly disagree. In fact, I suspect I never was.

Or maybe it's like this. The person who loved you no longer exists. I am a different being entirely. You would not recognize me if we passed each other on the street. And maybe that's why I found it so jarring to be transported so fully to that morning at Neptune Beach. And why I felt compelled to tell you, even though I'm not, really. Because I can't, of course.

Abbie just woke up and scratched my back for a second as she went into the kitchen to start the coffee. She asked me how I slept. She does this every morning. It signals the start of the day's official events.

Jesus fucking christ, I thought. If she dies first, I don't know how I'll ever get over it.

What are you doing, she asked me, measuring out the grounds. Who are you talking to in here?

Nothing, I said. No one.

Newlyweds

I hit my quota with the last sale of the shift, the receipts even out to the penny, and we finish inventory early enough to smoke weed by the dumpsters before I drive Miguel home.

We're at my car about to leave when we see the U-Haul driving straight at us. Stops just short of where we're standing. Two people jump out. The truck keeps running. They're newlyweds. It's the first thing they say to us. The next thing they say is that there is a man trapped in their U-Haul.

"A man?" I say.

"My ex," she says.

"I trapped him in there," the man says. He has a goatee. She has red hair. How do I say this? They look awful. Not ugly, just bad. Old food has this look. Dented. Sour. I can smell them in the late night wet of the mall parking lot.

"Like by accident?" I say. "Like he's locked himself inside?"

"Well," she says, pulling on her hair. "No." She looks over at the man with the goatee. "It's this whole situation."

"We're moving," the man with the goatee says. "Her ex heard about it and that's what set him off. He comes over, all fucked up. Corners me in the back of the truck."

"Threatening him," the redhead says.

"And then Tammy calls me from inside the house," the man says. "And I kinda duck past him to go check on her, you know? Then when I'm stepping down off the truck I get the idea to lock him inside. Just pops in my head. So I do it."

"Can y'all two go in there please?" Tammy says. "Our phones are with him in the back. Can't call nobody."

I pull out my phone. I look at Miguel. I tell the newly-weds to hang on. We take a lap around the U-Haul.

"Don't sound like there's a guy in there," Miguel says.

"He's biding his time," Tammy says.

"Are you sure about all this?" I ask the man with the goatee.

"Aw yeah," he says. "He's in there."

"Can y'all please go round there and open the door?" Tammy asks again. "He won't hurt nobody but us."

Miguel shakes his head. "I knew something fucked up was going to happen today."

I call the security firm that contracts at the mall and tell the dispatcher about the newlyweds in the U-Haul and the potential for a man trapped inside. She takes in every detail with an mhmm like she's been expecting this and my call just confirms what she already knows.

"Should we stay here?" I ask her.

"Who's we?"

"Nobody," I say. "We work at the cell phone kiosk."

"Well now we're definitely sending someone," she says. "Those roaming charges." She laughs.

"Ha ha," I say. "But we can go?"

"Well," the dispatcher says. "I'll be honest. That wouldn't look great."

* * *

The security guard who shows up introduces himself as Officer Perry. He stares at the truck, asks some questions, writes in his notepad. He doesn't have a gun. He makes sure to tell us this, like it'd be unfair if he did. He's wearing a sky-blue polo shirt. He is the shortest out of all of us and that includes Tammy. He wants to know more about the ex who is trapped in the U-Haul.

Hey You Assholes

"He's a dumbass," Tammy says. "If that tells you anything."

Officer Perry writes something down. "It does, actually."

Each of us are standing in a semi-circle around the back of the U-Haul. In the few minutes it took for Officer Perry to arrive, there's been no sound or movement coming from the truck at all. Officer Perry approaches, jingling the car keys the man with the goatee gave him, whose name turns out to be Dane. The security guard presses his ear to the door.

"He's dead," Miguel whispers to me. "They killed him." He stares at the truck. "There's a body in there. We're in danger."

"Can't hear anything," Officer Perry says, after listening.

"We're in danger," Miguel says again.

"Stop saying that!" Tammy says.

"I'm gonna just go for it." Officer Perry says. "Open her up. And then we'll just deal with it, okay? Okay everyone? We're just gonna set a perimeter, okay? Just get on back, please."

I am thinking about how the first thing they told us was how they just got married. Because it's wedding season, I guess. Or is it? Probably different for different places. "Like how a group of crows is called a murder?" I say to everyone as we retreat a few steps. "A bunch of weddings should be called a miracle." I am more stoned than I thought.

"What's he saying?" Officer Perry brings a hand to his ear.

"He's saying to be careful, I think," Miguel says.

"Don't worry," Officer Perry says. "I was in Iraq."

It keeps sticking in my mind that they're newlyweds because I am too. Last week. Except I haven't told anyone yet. We're not making a big deal about it. But it feels weird no one knows.

"Hey," I wave over at Miguel, who is watching Officer Perry approach the U-Haul door. "Did I tell you that Marta and I got married?"

Officer Perry unlocks and opens the U-Haul door. He shines his light in. He puts a leg on the bumper and hoists himself up. He pokes his flashlight around. "There's nothing in here," he says.

"What the hell," Tammy says, pulling her hair.

"That son of a bitch!" Dane says. "How he steal it all like that?"

Miguel and I jump into the U-Haul to see for ourselves. It smells like the newlyweds, only stronger. No body, no boxes.

"The strangest thing," Officer Perry says, picking something off the floor. He's holding a diamond ring pinched between two fingers. It sparkles in the glow of his flashlight. A thought passes through my head that it looks like the one I got for Marta, which doesn't make any sense because I didn't get her one at all.

"The engine's still running," Miguel observes.

The U-Haul door closes. We hear the lock click. Officer Perry drops the ring. The gears grind and we lurch into motion. Or maybe we start moving first and then he drops the ring. It's hard to tell because it's loud and dark and I don't know what's happening, but then again, I never do, do I?

Dumpster Cats

Gang all at the bar in their suits and ties and dresses and clacky shoes. Coming from Carter's sentencing is why so fancy.

Gemma, Carter's most recent whatever, openly sobs. Six months, she says. No one knows what to say to that.

Why Carter got six months is because he was getting bee-jed in St. John's Park after Birdie's last call when a patrolman spotlighted him and he took off running. It is worth noting that the individual doing the beejing was not Gemma, but someone else. A married someone else, who I know for a fact recently experienced a death in the family, her favorite aunt, and was not in control of her impulses due to grief and also because her husband is a known prick. As it happens, Carter is also a prick, but not because he ran or because he was getting beejed outside of his arrangement with Gemma. Because of something else.

The going rate for fleeing from police and resisting arrest with your johnson out in Jacksonville is six months. Or so goes the discussion from the gang at the bar.

Gemma pokes me. Were ya at the courthouse?

I shake my head. She's pretty blown out on something. Her makeup is all everywhere. She's new to this gang. I'm old to it.

Did Annie text ya or something? she asks and I shake my head again.

I'm just here because I'm here, I say. We worked together.

With Carter?

I nod.

At The Grotto?

The Grotto is this restaurant. Or used to be. No, I say. Alfred's. It was a salvage yard. Years ago.

Salvage? Gemma looks me up and down.

You know, I say. A junkyard. She's sending me signals, I think, or at the very least dangling it out there. What the hell. I smile at her.

A junkyard, she repeats back to me and I can hear the cylinders click into place when she decides to sniff me out, at least a little.

* * *

You don't like Carter, she says to me after some rounds. The rest of the gang has drifted. We have not.

No, I say. Not much.

She had been asking about what Carter was like when we were working salvage but up until now I hadn't been drunk enough.

It was this thing with the cat, I say, now drunk enough.

A cat, Gemma says.

I'm not some big cat guy or anything, I say. There were just so many. They helped out, ya know? Caught the rats. So we'd started putting food out and a couple of them got pretty friendly.

Cats, Gemma says.

Yeah, I say. Dumpster cats, but okay. Dumpster cats aren't so bad. In some cultures, dumpster cats are sacred.

Gemma nods. That's true, she says.

And there's one that's just very friendly. He's just this nice little guy. More than the others. So Alfred, or really his wife, scoops it up one day and takes it to the vet. Names it. Saves it, really.

Hey You Assholes

Names it what? Gemma says.

Well that's the thing, I say. Before she saved it, the cat was friendly to me in particular. And it was because I just happened to be the guy who would set out the bowls of food. It was one of my jobs. That's why. It's not like, ya know. What Carter said. Like I wanted to fuck the cat or something. Like he told everyone I put tuna fish on my balls or something. And I think he kicked it one time. But whatever. I set the food down. And this cat, it just preferred me.

God, Gemma says.

Yeah, I say, signaling for another drink and then pointing to Gemma's empty glass too. And this cat, there was this thing it did. Bowed its head kinda. Before eating.

Gemma shakes her head like she doesn't get it.

Well, I say. It would close its little eyes. Head down low. Ears back. I don't know. So the first time it happens, I go like, ya know, as a joke, I go, Amen.

No, Gemma says.

Yeah, I say. And then the cat starts eating.

No, she says.

Yeah, I say. But then the cat kept doing it. Every time. Closing its eyes. Bowing its head. Waiting for me to say

Amen. So I kept saying it. And like, we don't name the cats officially, but we start calling it Preacher, because of how he does that thing.

Preacher, Gemma says. That's good.

Yeah, I say. But then Carter starts saying he wants to kill one of the dumpster cats just because, ya know? Like, saying no one would care and nothing would happen. Messing with me, probably. But maybe not too, right? So I tell Alfred and he tells his wife and that's when Alfred's wife makes it official. No longer a dumpster cat. Now he's a house pet. And she names him Preacher from how all the guys called him that. Happy ending, right? Except not. Except a few weeks later, Alfred's wife brings Preacher to the yard while she helps with some paperwork and Carter, who was supposed to be repainting the road sign, sees Preacher, who was laying in the grass in the sunshine, and decides—for no good reason—to paint him.

Gemma doesn't say anything. I take a long drink. I've been shouting. I'm shaking a little. Painted him red, I say. From neck to tail.

I don't understand, Gemma says. Why would he do that?

For no reason, I say. Or maybe because he's a piece of shit.

Hey You Assholes

I finish my drink. She touches my wrist. We have come to an understanding.

The lights in the bar come on.

That piece of shit, she says.

* * *

I insist on driving her car. Because I'm a gentleman, I guess.

I'm still at my folks' place but you don't care, Gemma says in the passenger seat.

No, I say. I don't care.

We can go in through the side door, she says. And we can turn the TV on so they know I'm home safe. So they won't come down. But if they do come down, promise to be cool, okay?

She rolls down her window and lets the river stink in. What happened to Preacher? she says, taking off her high heels and putting her feet on the dash.

Well, we tried to wipe him off, I say. I mean, I tried to wipe him off. But ya know.

Crazy, she says.

He had eaten the paint or something. Trying to clean himself. He wasn't doing great. Kept throwing up. Big red globs of cat puke. Alfred's was way out there. Old Kings Road, if you know where that is. On the way to the vet— well, he just didn't make it.

Damn, Gemma says. Damn, damn, damn.

Of course Alfred fired Carter for it. But then Carter sued him for wrongful termination. For the unemployment. Kept getting rejected, but Carter kept opposing the judgment, which is a thing, apparently.

Gemma reclines her chair back. I'm just going to close my eyes for two seconds, she says.

Took it all the way to the state review where Carter was granted full payout. He ended up winning, I say. Can ya fucking believe that? He got paid. Legal fees too. But it didn't matter. He didn't get the whole thing. Alfred was wiped out. He sold to who knows. Wife left. Just a mess.

Gemma opens her eyes and tells me to turn right not at this stoplight but the next. This is me, she says after a few houses.

I park on the street and she leads me in through the kitchen. Dinner dishes in the sink. Some kind of pasta. She's got a room in the basement. She turns on the TV.

Hey You Assholes

In the end, I say and she shushes me.

In the end, I whisper. It was because in our employee agreement, it wasn't specifically outlined that we couldn't paint cats. That was the reason the labor board gave. Can you believe that?

I'm sitting on her bed and she's standing, facing her closet.

I'm going to put on my mermaid costume, Gemma says. It's from Halloween last year. That's when I met Carter and I looked so good. She puts her hands on her hips. I just want to be Ariel right now.

She digs the costume out from the bottom shelf in her closet and takes off her dress and steps into an ankle-length green sequin skirt. She asks me to fasten her shells.

A funny thing about Preacher, I say, hooking the clasp in the back as Gemma holds her hair up. Was that he had seven toes on one foot, which I learned is called polydactyly. He was just a special, special cat.

The zipper is stuck, Gemma says, struggling with the skirt. The more she pulls at it, the more green sequins she sheds on the carpet. She gives up. God, I'm such a cow, she says. She goes over to the mirror. God, I look like total shit.

I come up behind her. I hold her. Another funny thing about Preacher, I say, is that I started actually praying over his food, as strange as it sounds. At first it was just like, ya know, pausing, and then saying Amen, but then I started really praying. I mean, praying to *God*, weirdly enough. I'd be all like, dear God, bless these kitty kibbles so Preacher can do his kitty duty, kinda thing. Started as not so serious, but then turned into real prayer. I mean, what do you make of that?

Whatever Gemma had been on, she's coming off. I can see it leaking out of her. She's crying.

It's because I'm so fat, she says. It's all my fault.

I stroke her hair. It's not like I'm some big praying guy, I say. But hey it can't hurt either, right? I just felt like I was praying on his behalf, if that makes any sense. Like he was the religious one. I kiss Gemma on her neck, right below the ear. Is it weird that I still do it? I say softly. Pray for Preacher, I mean?

I'm going to kill him, Gemma says, wiping her face. She turns to me. We should kill him.

Make him eat paint, I say.

Yeah, Gemma says. But really murder him.

We move to the bed.

We can tie his hands down, I say.

Yes, she says.

Sit him down to a big bowl of red paint.

Yes, she says.

Teach him a lesson.

Yes, she says.

We hear footsteps creak overhead. We stop. I hold my breath. The toilet flushes.

Amen, I say.

Gemma reaches for the lamp. I find her in the dark.

Amen, she says.

A Cloud Place

The first time you flew in a plane was when your parents took you to Disney and it was so foggy when you touched down in Orlando, you thought the entire city was suspended in air, that Disney was in the clouds, because you'd been to other places, but by car, so you understood those places as car places, but Disney, Dad said, we'd have to take a plane, and that meant it was a plane place, a cloud place, and every day of the five days you were there, you couldn't believe how big it was, this cartoon come to life in the sky, this miracle made just for you, but as big as it was, there was an edge out there somewhere, a line that if crossed, you'd simply fall off and in the same amusement park, thirty or so years later, you'll wait for your girlfriend to finish the half marathon she's running dressed like the Little Mermaid, the event for which you had purchased an overpriced Prince Eric costume

online and when she gets through the chute, you had previously planned to make a clearing in the crowd and get
down on one knee, but back in January she kicked you out
of the house and even though she took you back after a
couple weeks, it really feels like the other shoe could still
drop, so you return the ring and throw away the costume
and instead of proposing, you hug her sweaty body and tell
her you're proud of her and buy her champagne and say that
you're sorry and will be so, so careful you don't fall off the
edge again.

Mr. Bananaman

"I'm looking for some friendly faces," he says, popping the lid off his coffee and blowing on it. "Some students—*former* students, only the brightest ones, just to, *you* know—and I'm not saying you think one way or the other about my situation, but the idea—my lawyer's really—was to have a few voices saying—not denying or defending, just *saying*—that okay, hey, is this guy perfect? No, not by a long shot, but what he also happens to be is a damn good high school physics teacher. So okay." He takes a sip of the coffee. "So that's what I'm asking."

"Mr. Menninger—"

"Please," he says, reaching across the table and touching my elbow. "Brian."

"Brian," I say, pulling back. "I don't—"

"Listen, do I need to tell you this? You weren't—I mean, I reached out to a bunch of other students before you. I guess

I'm kind of desperate? Ha ha. Not many takers, is what I'm saying. So far it's ah, let's see. No one and possibly you. Of course my lawyer was thinking it would help if it were, you know, more *recent* students. Don't think that because I asked other kids first that means you weren't a top student because obviously you were. I mean, c'mon." He points through the window to the car I arrived in, my mom's new silver Audi. "Big shot. You know, I see so many kids and it's always obvious who are the special ones. They're just *different*. Destined for bigger things."

I can tell by the way he's talking that he's waiting for me to cut him off or say thank you, but the thing is, I didn't have Mr. Menninger for physics in high school. He didn't coach any teams I was on and he didn't run any of my extracurriculars. In fact, the only direct interaction I can recall having with him prior to meeting at this Starbucks was during my first week of high school, fifteen years ago.

Mr. Menninger was supervising the lunchroom. He stood guarding the doors that went out to the courtyard. He kept flipping his walkie talkie in the air and catching it behind his back.

I didn't know his name. I just wanted to go home.

"Um sir?" I said after dumping my tray in the garbage. "I'm feeling pretty nauseous, I think?"

Mr. Menninger glanced briefly my way and then kept flipping the walkie talkie. "No, you're not," he said.

"Um, I'm not?"

Mr. Menninger hooked the walkie on his belt. "Well, I suppose you could be, but I highly doubt it. You see, *nauseous* means you make others sick. Like, if I were to look at you and feel queasy, then yes, you would be *nauseous*. But here I am looking at you and I feel fine. So you might think you're nauseous, but I suspect that you're actually *nauseated*, is that right? Tummy hurts?"

"I guess so?"

"See?" he said. "I further suspect you'd like to visit the nurse. For that you will need a pass." But then his walkie crackled and Mr. Menninger turned his back to answer. Still talking into the radio, he opened the door, walked across the courtyard, and disappeared around a corner. I waited in the doorway until another teacher asked what I was doing out of my seat.

It ends there, my memory. My only one of Mr. Menninger.

Best guess on why he's tracked me down is that Mr. Menninger has mistaken me for Derek, my best friend in high school, who *did* have Mr. Menninger for physics and who *did* have a lot of trouble initially and who *did* receive a fair bit of personal attention from Mr. Menninger during our junior year and who ended up not just acing the AP exam, but unlocking something significant inside himself and for that reason, Derek pursued the sciences in college—computers, I'm pretty sure—and after graduating, when Derek joined the Navy, his zeal and discipline helped distinguish his service as a helicopter pilot attached to a squadron that went on top secret missions around the world.

The reason I know this is because his mom told my mom, and my mom told me. Dinner last Sunday. My first after moving back.

"What are you trying to say?" I asked her.

"Well, I'm just saying how funny it is how you boys turned out so different."

"Not so different."

"Pretty different, I would say. Especially considering how you two did basically everything the same for so long."

"Okay well, not everything."

"Pretty much everything!"

"Our hair, you mean?"

"Oh my god, your *hair!*" My mom threw her head back and laughed.

In high school, Derek had piles and piles of curly brown hair—whereas I did not—and at the time, for whatever reason, one of the critical yet unspoken conditions of our best friendship was to endeavor to look as similar as possible. We had the same American flag t-shirt and the same clunky skate shoes and the same braided belt and the same single-strap black backpack and I begged my mom for a solid summer to let me get a perm so we could have the same hair too and against her better judgment—to hear her tell it now—she *let* me. Looking back I can see that okay sure, I looked completely insane, but more importantly to me—at least to the tenth grade version of me—the day after the salon, at the mall with Derek, someone at the food court mistook us for brothers.

Mr. Menninger continues to ramble in front of me and rips his napkin into little shreds. The more he talks about what it would mean if I spoke on his behalf, the more certain I am that he has me confused for Derek. "Before we get too far along," I say, stopping him mid-sentence. "I think I should—"

"What, you too?" Mr. Menninger crosses his arms. "You want the gossip column version of events? Well, that's not happening. Sorry. It's my personal life, dammit. That's what this whole thing is about. My *personal* life. And I get it. I do. I get why Mary Anne is gone and why my kids are—well, who knows. But all that is my personal life. I mean, why should it matter to the school board that the person I'm sleeping with isn't necessarily the same person I'm married to?"

"Well," I say. "When it's a student—"

"Former student! *Former* student!" Mr. Menninger looks over his shoulder and then points at me. "And here's something that's not in that article on STLtoday dot com or wherever you've read about this. Do you know how I met Mary Anne, my wife? No? Well, she was *my* teacher back in Berkeley. Not a professor. A TA, I guess they call them. This was the early eighties too. Quite the scandal. Now, I'm not saying this gives me a *psychological predisposition* or anything—except, hang on, maybe I am. Maybe that's something I need to be drawing more attention to. *Context.*"

"I don't think—"

"No, you're absolutely right," Mr. Menninger says, rubbing his chin. "What happened with Shannon is something I regret, really I do. I need you to know that. It was a mistake. It was *inappropriate*. That's the word everyone keeps using, by the way. You know why? Because they can't say *illegal*. Because it's not. In this state, an individual who reaches the age of consent may choose to sleep with her old physics teacher if she so wishes. Not that I'm so—well. You get it."

"I just don't know if I'm—"

"Look, Patrick, you wanna know the truth? They've got torches and pitchforks ready. I'm serious. Parents are *revolting*." Mr. Menninger drinks the last of his coffee and makes a face. "I know it's not a hearing. I know it's an execution. I just thought *someone* would say something. That someone would *want* to."

"I would, Mr. Menninger, really—"

"You would? Do you mean that? Because—God. I just. Oh man. That's great. That's just great, Patrick. So you're gonna go right before me, okay? The board president will ask if anyone has a statement or something to that effect and you'll just go up to the mic and say your thing, cool? Doesn't

Hey You Assholes

have to be more than a few sentences. Obviously the more detail and emotion you use the better, I think. Up to you, of course. Just—just *thank* you, okay? You don't know—well, I told you how much it means. So okay. Thank you."

He puts out his hand to seal the deal and there are these cold tingles near the base of my skull that I recognize as the unique combination of pity and shame and I know shaking his hand will make me complicit somehow but there I am, shaking it anyway, feeling Mr. Menninger's dry paper palm against my own and the only thing left to do is ask him where I should be, on what day, and what time he needs me to be there.

* * *

I've been gone too long with the Audi and my mom is waiting for me in the driveway.

"Here's my deal," she says, taking the keys. "I don't want to have a big thing every time you take the car. Let's not go back to *that*. So here's some growth. It occurred to me as I was waiting and texting and calling you that I didn't mention I was showing the Wilshire Terrace place to the Gaffneys today, did I? No, I didn't. No, of course not. Because it's been a pretty long time since I've had to tell someone else what my plans are, right? Same as you. Know what? I think this is one of our classic adjustment periods. So I'm in a rush now and maybe it looks like I'm frustrated or maybe I am just a little, but it doesn't mean that I'm not very, very happy that you're here with me now, okay?"

In the drawer with the stamps and paper clips and packs of gum, I find my mom's old address book. Derek's mom answers on the second ring and gives me his email. I use the old computer in the living room to send him a quick message and he responds before my mom is back from her appointment with the Gaffneys.

Hey man, he writes. *What are you doing right now?*

* * *

On the phone, Derek explains that The Atlantic Undersea Test and Evaluation Center—or AUTEC as everyone calls it—is located on Andros Island, which is somewhere in the Bahamas, about 300 miles south of Florida and the Department of Defense chose the spot due to its proximity

Hey You Assholes

to a two thousand-meter deep flat-bottomed trench that's surrounded on most sides by shoals and reefs and other smaller islands, making it the perfect sonar environment for submarines to practice good-guy-vs-bad-guy scenarios which would otherwise be disturbed by ambient ocean noise. Derek asks me to guess the name of the trench, but before I can think of anything he tells me it's called The Tongue of the Ocean.

"And it's called that because of—well, you can probably guess that too," Derek says.

"Um," I say. "Maybe—uh, salt content? The salinity?"

There is a pause and then some noises on Derek's end of the phone. "It's just shaped like a tongue, man."

"Ah."

"The shape of the trench. Looks like a tongue. I mean, topographically."

"Right, right."

"Salt content. That's just too—hey, what should I expect? Mom said you're some writer now."

I shift position and try to find my place among the decorative pillows on the living room couch. "No, that's—that's not correct. I'm an *under*writer. For loans. Banks. It's pretty boring."

"You wanna talk boring? We were only supposed to be out here for a week on this training thing with the submarine folks but something happened mechanically on those big—hey you ever see those big suckers? C130s? You know the aircraft? Well, something broke—*hard down*, they call it—and now we're just stuck out here. And yeah, they'll fix it eventually, but it's been ten days since we were supposed to be home and this is a small island. Like, there's nothing to do here but get fucked up—and Patrick, I mean *fucked* up."

I am back in the food court the day after my perm. The Sbarro's cashier pointing at me: *What does he want? Him, your brother. Yeah, ain't y'all brothers?*

"Like, there's just the one bar here, right? Normal base you'd have one for officers and one for enlisted. But here there's just this old dancehall. Cheap booze. Right on the beach. And every day—starting around 16 or 17 hundred— that's where everyone goes. Everyone, man. And that's the trouble, really." Derek stops. "Hey, that's my beer. Hey Anderson. No. Yours is over there. Yeah. Asshole." A pause. "Okay, what was I saying?"

Him, your brother. "The trouble," I say.

"Right," Derek says. "This thing last night. One of the new pilots—Danny O, we call him, because there's so many Dannys—anyway, we're all at the bar and it's late and everyone is blackout or on their way. And then this young thing, an aircrewman, starts dancing. I guess you'd call it a strip tease or whatever. Everyone is watching her, even me. Everyone, that is, except Danny O. He comes over to a bunch of us and starts on about how someone should take charge, put a stop to it. That as *officers* we should be repulsed by this kind of thing. Can you believe that? He says that we evolved as a *species* to find this display of promiscuity repellent—and Patrick? That is about when I stopped listening. I grab him by the shoulders and say, 'Danny, goddamnit, pull yourself together.' You know what he says? He's almost crying and he looks at me and goes, 'I think I love her, bro.' I know—I know! So I just go, 'Sorry man,' and punch him straight in the face."

"You what?"

"There's worse stuff going on, I promise you. Hang on, Patrick." He pauses. "What? Yeah, a buddy of mine." Another pause. "Huh? No, high school." Derek laughs. "Yeah, big time. Okay sorry about that. So what's up man? Don't even know how long it's been."

I tell him that however long it's been, it's been too long. I say that I'm back home for a little while without saying why and then adding it quickly like I almost forgot, ask if he remembers a teacher from our high school named Mr. Menninger.

"*Remember* him? I know about that whole thing. I mean, I've *heard* from him. No, really. Found me online a couple weeks ago. He's going around begging people to say he was this great teacher or whatever so he doesn't lose his pension."

"Oh right." The smell of the mall lingers from my memory. *Yeah, ain't y'all brothers?* "What did you say?"

"What did I *say*? Nothing. I didn't *say* anything. Oh you know what I *did* do though? I went and blocked him. Makes me sick to my stomach. Can you even imagine?"

I can imagine. I am imagining. Saliva floods the back of my mouth. I swallow.

"I mean, I used to go to him after school—yeah, you remember—and we'd be in his classroom alone. Like, no one coming in. I want to say that he'd close the door too. I think I definitely remember that. Who knows, man. Who knows what could've happened if—you know what? I don't even want to think about it."

"I heard—"

"I heard lots of things. Boys, girls, babysitters—some sick stuff. Are you in the—actually, be grateful you're *not* in this Facebook group. You'll sleep easier at night. Because if a fraction of this stuff is—well, let's just say they may have caught him with a student but—"

"Former student though, right?"

"Former, yeah. By about six weeks." Derek's tone shifts gear. "It was the summer after she graduated. He was *grooming* her. Jesus, Patrick."

I pull out the sticky note where I've written the details of Mr. Menninger's hearing. "Devil's advocate, I guess."

"Hang on," Derek says. "Okay, you're off speaker. Listen man, I gotta go but hey. I wanted to say something. I'm not gonna pretend like I don't know about your situation. Mom told me. Sounds like some dirty business. I don't know what I'd do if *my* wife—I mean, I know you've never met them, but Diana and the twins, they're why I do what I do, you know? What I'm saying is that I *understand*. And then Mom said you had a freak out at work or freaked someone out at work, or whatever. I just want to say that I *get it*, okay? You probably have other folks to talk to, but I was thinking, you know? How you'd come stay with us sometimes? Anyway, that's what I wanted to say. That I'm here for you."

I've been unfolding and refolding the sticky note. My hands are damp and the ink is smeared. Derek's voice glitches and warps. "Sorry, you cut out," He says after a few seconds, now sounding like he's at the end of a long hallway. "What did you say?"

The lights from my mom's new Audi flash through the bay windows of the living room. "Nothing," I say, putting the sticky note back in my pocket. "I didn't say anything."

* * *

Across the escalators from the arcade and down the corridor from the movie theater is the food court of Crestwood Mall. The pizza they serve disgusts my mom. She refuses to be within the radius of its smell. As a result, Sbarro's occupies a near occult fascination in my teenage mind. Whenever possible, I am compelled by a force I do not understand to eat there.

Standing in line the day after the salon, the chemicals from my new perm mix with the grease in the air in front of me. Derek orders pepperoni.

"What does your brother want?" the Sbarro's cashier asks him.

"Who?" Derek says.

"Him, your brother." She points to me.

"My brother?" Derek says, confused.

"Yeah," the cashier says. "Ain't y'all brothers?"

Derek turns around to look at me and for an instant, I see it. The same face my mom reserves for the pizza we're about to eat. There and then gone. A nanosecond, if that long. I lay awake at night as an adult man in the bed I grew up in and ask myself if it was there at all.

Derek punches my shoulder in the memory and laughs. "Yeah, sure," he tells the Sbarro's employee. "Course we're brothers."

* * *

On the day of the hearing, I am sitting next to Mr. Menninger on the chairs outside the conference room. The school board is inside but his lawyer is running late. Mr. Menninger is hunched over, elbows on his knees, typing something on his phone. He occasionally mutters *goddamnit.*

When the lawyer finally arrives, she's followed by a wobbly child hidden inside a big puffy coat. The lawyer takes off her gloves and sets down her briefcase and tote bag and backpack. She apologizes to Mr. Menninger. There appears to be a pen mark on her cheek. She shakes my hand. Her name is Paula.

"And this," she says, putting a hand on the head of the boy in the puffy coat, "is Lionel. Say hello Lionel. Oh c'mon buddy. No? Ah, that's okay. He's not—well, that's why we're a little late this morning. Not feeling so great, huh bud? No, we're a little under the weather." She turns to me. "You can keep an eye on him, right? For just a second?" Lionel slumps against the wall, playing with a toy banana. "Lionel, this is Mr. Stenhouse and he's—uh, he's going to tell you a story, okay? But Mommy's coming right back. Mommy's just going right in there, okay sweetie?" Paula takes a deep breath. "*I* will explain the delay," she says to Mr. Menninger, straightening her blazer. "Don't say a thing."

The click of the door closing echoes down the hallway.

I watch Lionel bend the arms and legs of his toy banana. "Who's your friend?"

He scrunches up his mouth and looks down. "Um," he says. "Bananaman."

"Hi Bananaman."

"Mr. Bananaman."

"Oh right," I say. "*Mr.* Bananaman."

Lionel tries to get the toy to stand on its own. It teeters then falls over.

"What can Mr. Bananaman do?"

He holds the toy out and shakes it around. "He can dance."

"Wow. You're right. He can."

Lionel looks at me and then back at Mr. Bananaman. He gets up and holds out the toy.

"You want me to have it?"

"*Hold* it."

I take the toy. He sits in front of me. "Can you say me a story on him?"

"About Mr. Bananaman?"

Lionel nods.

I look at the door to the conference room. "Okay, well. Maybe just a short one. So uh Bananaman—right, okay. *Mr.* Bananaman. He's dancing—he's a dancer, okay?" I hold the toy out and shake it like he did. "And he does such a good job dancing that he gets to dance in the, uh, the world championship of dancing, right?"

Lionel nods. "But then he gots in trouble."

"He did? Oh right. That's right. He did." I look the toy in the eye. "Mr. Bananaman got in very big trouble. Because, well. Hm."

Lionel raises his hand. "Maybe because Mr. Bananaman is sick and no sick kids can come to school sometimes?"

There is an exchange of muffled voices coming from the conference room. "Is that why Mr. Bananaman came with your mom today?"

Lionel nods.

"How does he feel now?"

"Um he feels okay now, I think," Lionel says, as his arms retreat into the sleeves of his big puffy coat. "But sometimes? At school? He gets really feeling *very* sick sometimes." He pulls his knees inside the coat too. He ducks his head so the collar covers half his face.

"That used to kind of happen to me too," I say.

Lionel sinks further into his coat so all that's sticking out is his hair at the top and his sneakers at the bottom. "Does it still?" he asks from inside.

Mr. Bananaman is made from a kind of light foam plastic, one that can bend in all ways, be compressed into any shape, and then, upon release, slowly returns to its original form. I give it a squeeze. "Not really."

The door to the conference room opens. Paula sticks her head out. "We're ready to start," she says.

"I thought—do you want to talk first?"

She shakes her head. "No time."

"Should someone maybe be out here for—"

"He's fine. Lionel baby, are you okay out here alone for two seconds? Let's go Mr. Stenhouse."

I stand up. I follow Paula into the conference room and sit down where she points. The school board president explains why we're here. They call my name. Mr. Menninger turns around and gives me a thumbs up. I walk to the spot where they've set up a microphone and everyone's looking at me, except not like how I pictured it, not like that at all. They're whispering and pointing to something by my waist. I follow their eyes to discover I'm still holding Mr. Bananaman. Really squeezing him. Face bulging. Limbs twisted.

"Ha ha," I say.

Paula comes to take it from me, but I can't let go for some reason. She's saying, Mr. Stenhouse, please. I'm trying to relax my grip but it just won't work. Paula snatches Mr.

Bananaman away. Everyone's saying my name. This is what I was waiting for. A moment to turn it all around. To prove them all wrong. I put a finger up and smile to let them know that I'm okay, that I just need two seconds. My eyes connect with Mr. Menninger's from across the conference room for the briefest of moments and what surfaces in my mind is the memory of him in the cafeteria, flipping the walkie talkie and catching it behind his back. *But here I am looking at you and I feel fine*, he says to the boy in front of him who just wants to go home.

I take a step back from the microphone, put my hands on my hips, and bend slightly at the waist. With my eyes closed, I take a deep breath in, and, as quietly as possible, vomit a column of gray slime onto the patterned carpet of the conference room.

Hey You Assholes

On Drugs

I think you're in trouble, said the cactus plant.

I don't know, I said. I'm feeling pretty good.

Yeah well, said the cactus plant. I think that's the trouble.

A New Kind of Dan

In the photo in question, the girl is young, no more than nine, dressed as a bride. Her father, mid-stride, beside her in a tux. His goatee cropped close. His gray skin hangs. A tight-lipped smile below zombie blue eyes.

His name is Dan.

Dan from work.

Dan from the office softball league.

Different from the Dan with the desk near the lobby. Different from the Dan in charge of new business. Not Tall Dan or Airsoft Dan or Mormon Dan or Hockey Dan.

This is Regular Dan.

Something off with that photo though. Everyone agrees. And it's not the framing or the colors or the glossy finish.

Maybe just the way it was used, we think.

Front and center on the cover of the program. Key art, that's called. Next to the casket and outside the chapel.

We know why it was chosen. After all, we were there when it was taken.

Some Saturday last April at Blackburn Park. Quite a sight with all the dogwood blossoms. Those soft pink petals against cartoon clouds.

No groom awaits the pair in the photo. No reception planned for after. Regular Dan's daughter wasn't getting married. This day wasn't about her.

It was about the impending death of Regular Dan.

According to the email he sent to the whole company, it was about Regular Dan getting to do something he wouldn't otherwise get to do. On account of this newly discovered abnormal genetic thing, he wrote. This accumulation of harmful mutations. The point being he didn't have much time. His prognosis meant he'd never hike the Appalachian Trail. He'd never see his favorite team win the big game.

But there was one thing Regular Dan could do. He could walk his daughter down the aisle, even if she wasn't getting married.

That was the idea, anyway. A man's last request sort of deal.

Word got around. The school got involved. People started to wonder how they could help, what they could do for Regular Dan.

Different ideas were pitched.

Messages were exchanged.

A plan hatched over phone calls and emails.

The day before the aisle walk, a delegation from the office went to Regular Dan's house with balloons and a printed certificate. When he opened the door, we crowned him employee of the year. Not for work he had previously done, we explained, but rather for the work we're sure he would have done in the future.

"This is an enormous surprise," Regular Dan said, voice shaking.

But that's not all, we told him. We asked him to follow us outside. There we gathered an entire group. They assembled into a line, just as we had rehearsed.

First up was the man who edited a gardening magazine. He presented Regular Dan with the Liberty Hyde Bailey Award for Excellence in Recreational Horticulture.

"But my hedges—" Regular Dan said, before the magazine man cut him off.

"We know," he said. "You would have one day."

Next was the dean of the community college. He awarded Regular Dan a bachelor's degree in Business Administration. The dean opened the padded folder and wagged his finger. "Not honorary," he said. "The real deal."

It went on like that all down the line. By the time he was through with everyone, Regular Dan was a church deacon, a board member of several businesses, the alternate for a bowling team, an extra in the upcoming community theater production of Godspell, and the presiding grand marshal of the box car derby.

There would be a day named after him, the city manager promised. They'd hang his basketball jersey on the wall of the high school gym.

Regular Dan was moved to tears. He wept through his fingers. The athletic director covered him with a hug. Jubilation broke out. The librarian's bracelets jangled as she double pumped her fists in the air near the rear of the crowd.

And then the next day at Blackburn Park. The dogwood blossoms covered the ground. Someone raked a path between the folding chairs.

They had music and everything. Two photographers. It felt like a movie. And you know, everyone mentioned, at one point or another, there was nothing regular about the Dan who walked his daughter down the aisle that day.

It was a time in our town where miracles were possible. That was the party line in the weeks that followed.

Hadn't the McClorey boy walked away from that bicycle collision? What about the police scandal? Couldn't that have been far worse? And wasn't there always some toddler being saved from drowning? Those asteroids that come close and then bounce away?

We were certain something like that would happen. He would emerge from the struggle a new kind of Dan. We couldn't wait to welcome him back to our world.

Things didn't happen like that, of course.

During the funeral, we stare at the photo on the program and on the easel next to the casket of Regular Dan on that day in the park. It has gone from vaguely off to fully bothersome and somewhere during the scripture reading is when we see it. We don't know why we didn't before.

The photo contains a blue sky in the background, the edge of the backstop from a t-ball game, a few falling dogwood petals, and a dying man walking next to his daughter. She's the source of what feels so wrong. Her face, her smile. Though not a smile, exactly. A grimace, in truth. She is leaning forward and baring her teeth, bracing for something we can't yet see.

What Happens to Those Coyotes?

It was in the middle of the morning rush when Festus, looking more stomped on than usual, walked into Venice Cafe, flip flops despite the February snow, sunglasses despite the gray, and laid his head straight down on the marble bar. When I didn't acknowledge him, he grumbled something I couldn't hear over the hiss of the steamer wand. I finished making the cappuccino before I asked him to repeat it and that's when Festus lifted his face, took off his shades, and said that Nick was dead.

"Nick," I said. "Nick Brown?"

"Downtown Nick Brown," Festus said, his eyes glazing. "Can ya believe it?"

"Fuck, what happened?"

"You were there," he said. "You saw his face."

"No I wasn't. I didn't see shit."

A customer, a regular, someone who worked for the university, I think, waved his hand and informed me we were out of half-and-half.

"You were at Tellers," Festus insisted, as I refilled the carafe. "We saw you."

"No you didn't," I said. "I delivered dry cleaning last night."

"Jesus, you're still doing that?" Festus said. "I thought they fired you for the windshield thing."

"Well, they hired me back for some reason."

"Got damn. What's the Knob Gnoster route pay again?"

"Forty an hour," I said. "Hey, what happened with Nick?"

Festus whistled. "Forty, jesus…"

"Festus," I said, which is not his real name, just the town in Missouri where he's from. "What's going on with Nick?"

"Oh right," he said and told me that the previous evening he and Nick were in the back game room of the billiards place on the business loop for a quiet couple of beers and there was a dispute over which asshole's turn it was on the pinball machine, the sexy Jackbot one, and it was all because of that guy with the ponytail who was dating Christina now, that fucking douchebag who was practically begging for a swift punch in the face and Nick had the idea to give him just that. He and Festus waited in the alley and when the ponytail guy came outside to smoke, Nick sprung from a shadow and swung a wild fist, clocking him on the temple. A direct hit, except, they realized, it wasn't Christina's new boyfriend, it wasn't the guy with the ponytail. Or rather, it wasn't the guy with the ponytail they had meant to punch in the face. It was a different guy with a ponytail. An older guy. A bigger guy. And this ponytail guy was extremely pissed off on account of getting punched in the face for no reason, as you might imagine. And so, to keep the guy from calling the cops, Nick offered his own face to be punched, which the guy took him up on.

"And when he does it, it's like that old joke," Festus said. "Two hits, the hit to the face and the hit to the floor. Nick, man, when he came to, he was all scrambled. Couldn't walk straight, stopped talking mid-sentence. Looked like a video buffering."

When he saw how messed up Nick was, ponytail guy felt bad for hitting him so hard and offered to share his coke, which they did off the back of his hand in the alley and for a little, it seemed to sort Nick out. They did a couple more bumps and walked to Tellers where they drank a little, nothing crazy, before saying goodnight.

"And now Nick's not answering his phone," Festus said. "And like, I was just up at his place. I mean, I banged on his door so loud that people down the hall were yelling."

All this time, I had been making drinks like a mad man and finally cleared the busiest part of the Sunday crowd. I pulled a quad shot of espresso and picked out a day-old bagel to dunk in hummus. I took my break on the stool next to Festus.

"He's probably just hungover," I said, chewing.

"He's dead," Festus said, head on the bar again. "He's all pale and shit right now in his apartment, man. I can see him. I just know it."

"So what now? Cops?"

"No." Festus lifted his head and rubbed his chin. "I don't know. No cops. Not yet, I guess."

"He'll probably walk in here in the next five minutes," I said. "And then won't you feel like a dumbass."

But he didn't. Every time the door opened, Festus would pop his head up and scowl when it wasn't Nick.

"What are you doing now," Festus said to me at the end of my shift.

"Counting the drawer."

"After, I'm saying. Hey man, I'm freaking out over here, okay?"

I checked my watch. "He's just sleeping it off. It's not even noon. You know what? He's probably over at Duffie's. He's probably smoking with Duffie. Or Jane. They're probably back together. He's probably gone to her place."

"Let's go over there, then," Festus said. "I mean, let's go over to Duffie's. I got business with that guy anyways. He owes me a hundred bucks. A hundred bucks at least."

"He's not paying you for that bike, man."

"We'll see," Festus said. "We'll just fuckin see."

Festus followed me out the door. He smoked a cigarette on the walk to where I had parked. He put the butt out on the bottom of his flip flop before getting in the laundry van. "They let you keep this thing overnight?"

"Only when I work days back to back."

Festus shook his head. "You know what's sad? You got like, three jobs. Work all the time. And yet you're always broke."

Hey You Assholes

"I don't know where any of it goes," I said. "That's the worst part."

"The worst part, jesus," Festus said. "I don't even wanna think about the worst part."

* * *

Duffie's apartment was one of a dozen in a single story complex on the east side of town. He sold weed through the winter and worked roofing with me in the summer. He was the only white guy with dreadlocks that didn't annoy the shit out of me. In fact, I respected him a great deal. You just couldn't shake him. He was like our little Buddha. He didn't even mind that Festus and I woke him looking for Nick. He put on a pink fuzzy robe and said he should be up anyway. He sat on the couch and packed a bowl and took in a lungful. Behind the smoke, Duffie smiled and passed the glass piece to me.

"Downtown Nick Brown?" he said. "Haven't seen him since before Christmas. Didn't he go to California or some shit?"

"He came back, I guess," I said.

"How's she treating you," Festus asked him, pointing to the vintage ten speed leaning against the wall.

"Don't start, dude," Duffie said. "Here, try this. New stuff."

"If you're trying to distract me, it's not working," Festus said, taking the pipe. "You owe me and you know it."

"I'm sorry you don't remember giving me that bike, brother," Duffie said. "I truly am. But the fact is, you did give it to me. And I tried to give you money at the time but you refused. That was three months ago, and now, well, now it's my bike. And I'm not giving you money for something I own. Those are just like, my principles."

"You're a drug dealer," Festus said. "You don't have any principles."

"Don't be an asshole," I said to Festus.

Duffie smiled. "I'm not a drug dealer. I simply help my friends out every once in a while."

"Well, I'm not your friend," Festus said. "Or whatever. I'm not your friend anymore."

Duffie clicked his tongue and bound his dreadlocks under a floppy cloth hat. "You don't mean that."

"I mean it alright," Festus said. "Oh I fuckin mean it so hard."

"You don't have Jane's number, do you?" I asked Duffie.

"The tires are flat," Festus reported of the bicycle, squeezing along the wheel. "You don't even ride—jesus—have you ever ridden it? Jesus christ, man."

I had a ten-minute conversation with a girl who turned out to be the wrong Jane while Festus performed a diagnostic review of the ten speed's components and frame. Duffie sprayed water on the fronds of a giant green plant that was blooming with bright yellow buds. He occasionally snapped off a few of the flowers and ate them, working it over in his jaws before swallowing.

When I hung up the call with not-the-right-Jane, Duffie offered to guide us to what he believed to be the right-Jane's apartment complex in Kelly Ridge. When I asked him how sure he was that she still lived there, that she was the right Jane, he packed a new bowl and smoked contemplatively.

"Seventy five percent," he said, passing the pipe to Festus. He snapped off a couple more yellow flowers. "Paracress. The toothache plant. Here."

I chewed up a couple flowers and a numbing sensation flooded the back of my mouth. Festus ate some too but said he couldn't feel anything.

"That means it's working, ding-dong," Duffie said, smiling.

* * *

Festus was lying down, stretching out in the second row of the laundry van. "I won't miss him, honestly. Been getting on my nerves for weeks."

"Who?" Duffie said.

"Nick, man."

"We don't know that he's dead," I reminded them. "We don't know anything. He's probably, well, he's probably fine."

"Probably," Festus said. "Lots of things are probably."

Duffie pointed to a gated entrance. "This is it."

"Jane, Jane, I'm trying to think," Festus said as we parked in one of the visitor spots. "Did I even know this Jane? What does she even look like, Carson?"

Jane was still an undergrad, a sorority wash out. The first time I met her she told me a story about how she was depressed in high school because she didn't have enough loose skin to pierce for a belly button ring. She asked me if I could imagine that kind of sadness, that kind of isolation. She told me I will never know the loneliness of the skinniest girl in class. She looked exactly like that one girl from Dawson's Creek, but when I told her that, Jane scoffed and said everyone says that and then didn't talk to me again for the rest of the party.

"You know her," I said. "She hung around this summer. Looks like a regular girl but all stretched out."

"Anyone want this?" Duffie asked, holding out the piece.

"She is way taller than Nick too," I said, taking the pipe. "They made a funny couple."

"Okay, I kinda remember. Nick liked tall ones," Festus said. "One thing you could say about the man. He had a type. Giraffes with makeup. A long string of extremely tall girlfriends."

"Girlfriends," I said.

"Well, not girlfriends, I guess," Festus said, the bowl glowing. "Me, I like the short ones, you know? I like it when they scramble all over you like a monkey."

"I like that too," Duffie said.

"Fuck you, Duffie," Festus said. "Bike thief."

"You win, man," Duffie said. "Take it back. You can have it. I don't want the damn thing anymore."

"That's not the point, asshole."

"Hey, remember Stein?" I said. "That guy from sopho-more year?"

"The suicide?" Duffie said.

"No, that was the kid from Alaska," Festus said. "Stein, Stein. What happened to him?"

"Choked on his puke, they said."

Something sinister descended. We were quiet for a moment as it made the rounds. The heater in the van sputtered and I pounded the dash above one vent until the noise stopped.

"Jane, Jane, she waxes and wanes," Duffie sang softly, glassy-eyed. "She waxes and wanes, my sweetest of Janes. Hey, did you hear that? I just made that up."

I tried the bowl but it was cashed. "Know her unit number?"

"Hmm," Duffie said. "I do not."

In the backseat, Festus tried Nick's phone a few times. "Still straight to voicemail," he said, shaking his head.

"Yo, if I'm being totally honest," Duffie said, grinning. "I sort of forgot what we were doing here."

"I think that's her," I said, pointing to a girl getting out of a red sedan.

But it wasn't. And none of the cars in the parking lot looked like what we remembered was Jane's. And then one of us just started saying her name. Jane, Jane, Jane. And then each of us said her name in an escalating spiral of intensity until we were shouting ourselves hoarse and no one came out to tell us to be quiet so we did it for a long time, longer than you think three people can scream at the top of their lungs without anyone rushing to see what's the matter. Jane, Jane, Jane. We chanted like that until I had to go back to work.

* * *

Duffie and Festus couldn't decide where I should drop them off so instead they just came with me. At the laundry, they helped me load in the packages of freshly dry-cleaned Air Force uniforms under the supervision of Yolanda the weekend manager, who looked confused as to why there were two people accompanying me, but didn't speak enough English to ask me about it.

"Cuidado," she said, waving to us from the loading dock and pointing up at the sky.

"What's she saying?" asked Duffie.

"That's like, her little name for me," I said, driving away.

We had just passed through Boone County when it started to rain. Or not rain, I guess. Sleet.

"Glad you're the wheelman in this." Duffie was propped up against a laundry cart in the back. "Whew, this looks miserable."

"Been in worse," Festus said. "One time, driving back from Lawrence. Way worse than this."

"Try Nick again, man," I told Festus. "He's gotta be up by now. You know what? He's probably fucking with us. Laughing his ass off that we went looking for him."

"Nah man." Festus had moved from the second row to riding shotgun and was staring out the window. "That dude is not laughing his anything off."

"That was our exit," I said. "I cannot see shit."

Halfway to Whiteman Air Force Base, the temperature dipped and the sleet froze and the laundry van started fishtailing across the double yellow lines of state road 127.

"Holy shit, you almost went off the road there," Festus said.

"Nah, I'm okay," I said.

Duffie took a seat and buckled himself in. "This feels, uh, pretty dangerous, I think."

The van slowly rotated sideways. "Yeah, okay," I said. "I agree with that, I guess."

The wheels started to spin out with every slight acceleration. Even going as slow as I reasonably could, I was not in control of what was going on. Approaching a turn, I yanked on the emergency brake and we drifted. The rotors screamed.

"Not a fan of that noise," Duffie said. "Not a fan one bit."

"Shut the fuck up," I said, turning off the radio. "Everyone just needs to shut the fuck up for a second, okay? We just have to make it to Dunksburg. I've stopped there before."

We drove at a snail's pace on the slick chip seal until we got to the town. There was a diner open, thankfully, but inside felt like the last moments of a party of some kind. Empty food trays on the counter. Balloons floating a few inches off the floor. The couple people standing around were dressed in funeral black. Men in somber suits, women in simple dresses. The air stunk of cigarettes and a sign was hung on one wall that said in big block letters, OTIS, OUR

BELOVED FRIEND. There were bouquets of white flowers on each table.

"Holy shit," Festus said.

"Don't say it," I said. "Don't say anything."

A woman approached us, frowning. "Private party tonight," she said. "Sorry boys."

"But we're here for the event," Festus said.

"No, we're not," I said. "I'm delivering laundry to Whiteman." I showed her my CDL and vendor paperwork that gave me base access. "The roads are getting really bad. We just need—"

"We lost someone today too, okay?" Festus cut in. "That's why we're here. Pay our respects. We're sorry for being late, but we just found out."

"You all reek of weed," she whispered, looking at Duffie. "You know that?"

A tall man holding a half-filled glass tumbler came over and put a hand on the woman's shoulder. "Vera," he said, bobbing slightly. "I told you. Everyone is welcome at this table."

"They said they're here to pay respects."

The man had rosy cheeks high above a mossy smile. "Then let them do that."

She pointed to Festus. "This one's in flip flops."

"Vera," the tall man said. "They belong here too."

He gestured for us to sit at a booth where he poured a little bourbon into three plastic cups and then raised his glass in a toast and we drank them all off in a shot. The tall man wiped his mouth. His eyes were mineral blue and bloodshot. "We're telling stories, that's what we've been doing, telling Otis stories all night. Well now. You're dry over there. Here's a little more then. A little more for all around." We drank again. "How did you know him from?"

"School," Duffie said, sipping.

"He was on our floor freshman year," Festus said. "We all had econ together."

"Ah yes." The tall man refilled our cups again. "Our Otis was a scholar, was he?"

"Well," Festus said. "Not to speak ill of the whatever, departed, but he was maybe… I dunno. He thought he was smarter than he really was, I guess."

The tall man laughed until he coughed. He took a drink and looked down at his lap. "I wish… I guess I didn't really know him. Not as a man, I didn't. I thought I did, but I didn't. Because, well, you see, I was so much older when he was born. And I guess it was hard to be a brother like that. I know he had trouble in school early on. That I remember. But I always thought of him as crafty, if not book smart. Just had a sense about certain things."

"Crafty," Festus said, snapping his fingers. "That's exactly the word I'd use. Shrewd."

"Cunning," Duffie said.

"You." The tall man pointed at me. "Are you from school too?"

I took a drink. "Yes."

"And what's your Otis story?"

"Uh," I said. "I don't know. I guess he was just—I mean, he was just part of the group."

"Part of the group." The tall man nodded. "Isn't that something?"

"He wanted to be a doctor, I think," Festus said. "Always talked about being a brain surgeon. Didn't he say that all the time, Carson?"

"A doctor, yeah," I said.

"He would have been a fine doctor," the tall man said. "By all accounts. Because, by all accounts, he was a good friend. To you, yes, but to his, well, to his fellow man too.

Hey You Assholes

So thank you, boys, you men, I'm sorry, of course. Thank you for coming. Thank you for sharing these treasures with me. That's what they are, that's what I want. I just wished… I need—"

The tall man put his head in his hands. A trio of moles showed through his thinning hair. The black rain lashed the windows. I closed my eyes and saw Nick on his bathroom floor, rigid, blank-eyed, mouth open. He was dead, that much I knew. Such a waste. And so young too. And we'd say the same thing in five years when it happened again. Maybe it wouldn't even take that long. Maybe it would be me.

* * *

But it wasn't. I would get out of that scene alive. I didn't deserve to, but that's just what happened. Don't look at me like that, I didn't have anything to do with it. I was simply playing out the rest of the string. Or no, that's not right either, not right at all.

And anyway, Nick didn't die. Not that night. He had just lost his cell phone and a headache kept him in bed until evening. We saw him after the roads were salted and we finally made it back, at Addison's around one in the morning for industry happy hour. He was just sitting there at the bar, watching hockey highlights with double black eyes, drinking a beer. Festus screamed. Duffie broke out in a little hippy dance. It was, I think, a kind of miracle. We told everyone about how he had been resurrected.

It sticks out to me now because Nick did die later that year. A car accident, of all things, while visiting his dad in Myrtle Beach. But by that time, Festus had moved away and Duffie had been busted for selling peyote and I had been fired from the laundry again, this time for something so stupid you wouldn't believe me if I told you.

So maybe it's like this, like in the cartoons. How the coyote keeps running after overshooting the cliff? Eventually he falls, but what if he didn't? I guess what I'm saying is, I think it's still possible. Tell me, you fucker, what happens to those coyotes? They exist, I bet, of course they exist. Shit, I thought I was one, I thought we all were. And so what do I do with the rest of my life now that I know I'm not?

Hey You Assholes

Roller Coaster House

Six weeks after I move back in, my wife wants to buy a house. Specifically, this house she found on the internet. She says it's a roller coaster house and by that she means there is a roller coaster in the backyard, the next lot over. She shows me the listing and asks if I can believe it. Says that part of the track goes right over the roof. Says that at the asking price it's still a great deal. Says that even though we don't want kids it matters that the schools are good because that factors into future appraisals of the roller coaster house. Not that we'll ever move. Just that we may want to consider refinancing at some point. Use the capital to reinvest into the roller coaster house.

She waves her hand around in the air like a wand. "A sunroom," she says. "A man cave, maybe."

I tell her I don't want a man cave, but she says of course I do. I ask her how serious she is about this whole thing and she says extremely serious.

Against my better judgment, I agree to attend the open house for the roller coaster house. The open roller coaster house, my wife says.

Looking for a place to park, my wife points out that the roads have recently been sealed. She pokes my shoulder. That thing with the potholes last year, she refuses to let it go.

"Very smooth," I say.

"Only joking," she says.

The house itself seems fine. The shingles are new, the realtor points out from the lawn. She hands me a pamphlet with all the details. It's got central air, hardwood floors, a working fireplace, etc.

And of course the roller coaster in the backyard.

"It's always going like this?" I ask the realtor, gesturing to the old-fashioned wood track. "There's no off season?"

"That's right." She has some lipstick on her teeth. "Even on Christmas!"

I ask her why the current owners are moving and she gives me a look like ha ha, very funny, asshole.

Hey You Assholes

Inside, there are other couples wandering around the rooms. We are looking to answer the same question and the answer is yes—yes, in every corner of the house, you can hear the roller coaster. The clacking of the track, the cranking of the chains, the delighted woos of her passengers. My wife says it's not as loud as she thought it would be but she has to say it three times before I can hear her. One of the other husbands watches this exchange and smirks at me and I surprise myself by briefly imagining choking him to death.

"What do we think?" my wife says in the car, driving back.

"Honestly," I say. "It's very unique."

"Honestly," she says, chewing her lip. "I need this, okay?"

I say okay, jeez.

Later that night, we make an offer on the roller coaster house. It is more money than we have currently or could hope to have in the near future. My wife says that real estate is about long-term investments. You know what they say about land, she says, about how god's not making any more. And I say, he's not? But she doesn't hear me. At least she's acting like she can't. And anyway, it doesn't matter because we discover the following afternoon that our offer to buy the roller coaster house has been declined. The realtor tells me about this older couple, retired Utahns. Amusement park enthusiasts, apparently. Came in with cash and bid over asking.

Upon hearing this news, my wife rushes out into our backyard and I go after her. She is facing our fence, looking at where the roller coaster would be, if only we had one. Instead there is just another house, very similar to the one we're renting. She is crying a great deal.

"We'll find some other funky house," I promise her. "There's all kinds, I bet. A house next door to a zoo? What about that?"

"No," she says. "That would be a nightmare."

And right then, that's when it really starts. Something like love at first sight except in reverse. The beginning of the end. I can still see it. I can still smell it. Goddamn it. Our little backyard. The khaki grass. The space where a roller coaster should have been.

There were other things, of course. Bigger things. Lying and cheating. And smaller too. Laundry left in the washer. Sandwich crumbs on the couch.

But the roller coaster house. I almost forgot. The first of many chances I had to turn it all around.

Hey You Assholes

Cullen

As a defensive measure, Cullen had taped garbage bags to his windows. Black ones. Double layered. He'd been awake since Tuesday. Hadn't left the house since Friday.

He told me all this in a calm voice. Maybe a little amused by himself. It didn't sound like he was having a psychotic episode, but even Cullen had to admit some of the evidence was pointing in that direction.

He was calling to ask me if he was going crazy.

"I'm going to send you a link to a teaser video, okay?" Cullen said. He asked me to watch it while we were still on the phone.

Just seemed like a normal movie trailer to me. They make a few like it every year. Guy moves back home and gets involved with an old girlfriend. Other stuff too, but that was the main gist.

"Okay," I said. "I watched it."

"A little obvious, isn't it?" Cullen said.

He started talking about parts of the video I didn't remember and I realized he thought the movie was about him. That the producers of the film were *mocking* him. And didn't the lead actor look a little too familiar, he asked? Basically cast his twin. And Cullen explained how the main character, this handsome scoundrel, goes on to be humiliated and destroyed by the deranged freakazoids that control local law enforcement and political leaders and education centers. And wasn't that convenient, narratively, he meant?

"It's a message," he said. "A warning. You see it, right?"

Before this phone call, I hadn't spoken to Cullen in years. The last time was when he was in town visiting friends on his way up to a small university in Vancouver. We met for drinks. His divorce was fresh. This position as guest lecturer fell in his lap at just the right time, he said. He told me about testifying in front of a congressional subcommittee in his capacity as a new media expert. He told me about working for a creative branding agency in Los Angeles and where he was when he got the news he was being laid off. Smoking a doobie in an alley in North Hollywood with Quentin Tarantino, he claimed.

I had repeated these stories to friends at work. Some people had heard of him before. He had a Wikipedia page. What can I say? I was proud to know him.

"I know you see it," Cullen said on the phone.

I was trying to think what I would want to hear from an old friend if my brain was coming apart, but I wasn't firing on all cylinders myself. Audrey and I had one of our knock-down-drag-outs and as a result I was staying in Lewis's spare room. Couldn't decide whether this was really the end or we'd fix things eventually.

I was distracted, is what I'm saying.

"I do," I told Cullen. "I see it."

"I got into some trouble up here, man," he said. "Old habits. *Bad* habits. I don't know how much they told you, but I got into some very heinous shit."

I assured him no one told me anything and he scoffed like he didn't believe me.

"It was the club scene, really," Cullen said. "The ones up here? *Outrageous*. Can't describe it. Won't even try." He paused. "And there was some meth too."

In college Cullen had floppy movie star hair and this big hero jaw and he was tall and had good teeth and on top of those things he was also quite brilliant. Not my words. That's Professor Hodges. She taught Intro to Ancient Greece and was also in love with Cullen a little bit, I think. Nothing too romantic. She was just in love with him in the way we all were back then. He was that kind of person. She let him stay in her house out in Bonnie View between semesters. One day we ate a bunch of shrooms at her place and I sat at Professor Hodges' piano, silently crying onto the keys and after what felt like a long time Cullen came over and hugged me and we dragged this old canoe to the pond behind the house and paddled around the milky green water and when I looked up, the trees had turned into kindly old gentlemen. They were skeletons but nice ones and they were reaching down with their branches to give us a million kisses. I know it sounds scary but it really wasn't.

Maybe there was a place like that Cullen could go now, I thought.

"Can you get out of the city?" I asked him. "Unplug for a little?"

Cullen laughed. "They'd find me this fast." I could hear him snap his fingers. "You don't know how much power they have."

Hey You Assholes

I wasn't sure if I should ask who "they" were. I didn't want to encourage him but I also wasn't ready to puncture his delusion, if that's what this was. I began to realize that whatever was happening might require a professional. Someone who was closer to Cullen both physically and emotionally. What could I really do? I was in a different country, sitting on a concrete bench in an open-air shopping mall. That's where I was when Cullen called me. People walking all around and into the stores and carrying bags. Could any of them help? And what was the problem, really?

"Did you hear that?" Cullen asked me. "That click on the line?"

Said he needed to get off the phone right away. I made him promise to call me back in an hour.

I went into The Cheesecake Factory and sat at a high top. Muted basketball played on the bar TV. Two men at the far end watched the game. We drank beer in silence and I thought about my situation.

I had been with Audrey long enough, had split like this enough times, that I was familiar with the script of what came next. My tearful apology. Her begrudging acceptance. It all felt so corny.

I went out to call Cullen. It had been over two hours and was fully dark then. There was a playground in the park across the street and I wandered over to sit on the swings. A cold wind was picking up over the ridge.

No answer from Cullen. I tried Audrey instead.

"How is Lewis's house?" she asked, which annoyed me because she knew exactly how Lewis's house was from the last time we had done this.

"Fine," I said. "How's my house?"

"Oh," she said. "So you called to fight."

In truth, I didn't know why I called. I imagined a squirming black grub in my brain. That Cullen had somehow infected me. And Audrey was the person I chose to say the one thing in the universe that would kill the virus and make everything better. Bullshit, really. Beer thoughts. "Do you remember my friend from college?" I asked her. "Came to visit once? You picked us up from that tiki bar."

"Um," she said. "Maybe?"

I was suddenly exhausted by the prospect of explaining it all. "Never mind then."

Audrey asked me if I was okay. I told her I was. I smelled someone grilling in the housing development next to the

Hey You Assholes

park. That's what I thought it was at first. It took me a few minutes to put it all together. Something white started to fall from the sky.

Snow, I thought. Strange.

Except of course it wasn't snowing. This was Southern California. The grilling smell was wildfire smoke and the snowflakes were ash.

"There's a fire down here," I said to Audrey.

"Oh Tuna." That was her name for me when she was done being mad. "I think you should come home."

I called Cullen a few more times from the parking lot. No answer.

On the radio they were announcing the first wave of evacuation orders. I joined a wall of brake lights on the 101 going north. Tried the PCH but it wasn't any better. Worse, even. People were stopped and pulled over on the shoulder and walking around and chatting. There was news making its way through the mass of traffic. The fire had jumped the freeway. Apparently, somewhere up ahead there were drift-wood beach cabins completely engulfed.

"Sounds like we're trapped," I said to a man in a cowboy shirt and boardshorts.

"Wouldn't that be something?" he said, laughing and walking away.

On the ridge above us, the wildfire formed a line of red scallops. My eyes watered from the smoke as I watched them slowly chew their way down the mountain. The wind gusted. I could feel the heat. My phone lit up. Cullen calling back.

"I'm at the hospital," he said. "I had a moment of lucidity and I seized it and I'm safe and I'm at the hospital. I have to surrender my phone, but I wanted to call you first. Because I know how I sound right now and I'm just very sorry about it."

"Good," I said. "That's really good, Cullen."

"I'm pretty sick this time, they're saying. I think they might be right. But I'm just—well, I just wanted to ask. You don't think any less of me?"

"No," I said. "Not one bit."

"If I get married again, I'm inviting you," he said. "I just wanted to say that. I won't forget this."

The man in the cowboy shirt tapped my shoulder. Another update. They had cleared a path and wanted everyone back in their cars. I told Cullen that I had to go, but he wasn't there anymore. He had already hung up.

Hey You Assholes

The column of traffic crawled forward. We passed burning palm trees and balls of flaming chaparral that bounced along the sand and extinguished in the ocean.

All that fire and chaos. The burn scar would be visible for years. The drive should have taken thirty minutes and ended up taking three hours. When I arrived back home, my nerves were shot. I fell apart in Audrey's arms. Not my usual ritual of begging forgiveness. This was something else. I was overcome with the sense of a tragedy having been averted. A near miss from a larger darkness.

It distracted me from what was really happening. The way Audrey didn't grip me back. Didn't stroke my hair. And how the little arguments picked right back up the next day.

The wildfire went on until we got rain and then there was so much rain it became a problem. The mudslides did the real damage. The wildfire just cleared the way. The debris chutes were overloaded and big boulders came smashing through rooftops with no warning whatsoever. Unprecedented, they said on the news. A dozen people died and somewhere around then is when Audrey and I split for good. I never heard from Cullen again, though there's still time, if he's out there.

As for me, I am doing about the same. I survived a wild-fire and a mudslide and falling out of love and all kinds of stuff that had every right to kill me. You'd think I'd be smarter, but I'm still essentially the same asshole making the same mistakes.

I still catch myself thinking things can't get any worse.

PART THREE

Everyone wants to hear the horror stories.

At This Week's Meeting of the Young Mountain Movers

At this week's meeting of the Young Mountain Movers, there would be no talk, Pastor Matt said. Instead, we would be doing an exercise. This, he said, gesturing to a circle of chairs in the center of the room covered with brown butcher paper and held together with painters' tape, was The Cave.

What's in there, Robin Dernberger asked.

The answer, Pastor Matt said.

The answer to what, Greg Horne asked.

To the only question there is, Pastor Matt said.

We went into The Cave and sat down in a circle. The Youth and Community Center was newly constructed and the smell of fresh drywall lingered in the air and mixed with our breath and body smells inside The Cave, which from inside and under fluorescent lights, did not look brown, but gold. Pastor

Matt tugged his ball cap low and opened in prayer. He led us in singing a church song and then another one. After he put his guitar down, he looked up at us with shiny eyes.

Right now there are kids just like you trapped in a cave just like this.

Just like this? Jeremy Howser asked, poking at the brown butcher paper.

On the other side of the world, Pastor Matt said. He told us to close our eyes. Now imagine it. You're all just messing around with your coach, and that's me, I'm your coach and, we're all a team of some sort, okay? And we do this all the time, just explore together. Except this time, it happens in a way where we can't leave, so now we're trapped and we can't, you know. Get out.

I can get out, Greg Horne said, lifting a corner of the butcher paper.

I can too, said Jeremy Howser, trying to peel off the painters' tape without tearing it. Sorry, he said, tearing it.

Pastor Matt reminded everyone that our eyes were supposed to be closed and described our surroundings and how dire our situation was. Do you feel it, he said, his voice shaking slightly. How close death is in this place? Can you smell its sulfur breath? And it's, well, it's just very uncomfortable too. Cold. Wet. You're miserable, is what it comes down to. I mean, there's really no hope. So every breath is one more closer to, you know, dying, and I mean, that fact is staring you right in the face. So now you're basically panicking, right? And remember death's hot breath? Well, it's closer now and—

Greg Horne interrupted by making a long and loud farting sound with his palms and lips. Pastor Matt bowed his head and waited for the laughter to peter out. He looked around at each of our faces and smiled thinly.

See, now, I'm actually glad you did that. Because that's one way to deal with it, I suppose. Like it's all a big joke. But tell me, Greg. What do you see when you close your eyes? Hm? What special treatment do your farts buy you in The Cave? Think about it, I'm serious.

None, I guess, Greg Horne said after thinking about it.

None, Pastor Matt repeated with his eyes closed.

Pastor Matt, Robin Dernberger said.

Yes, he said, his eyes still closed.

Pastor Matt, my mom is doing the snack this week? And um, she texted me that she's here? And that she needs help carrying all the Taco Bell and that she's parked in the loading zone out back?

Darn it, Pastor Matt said, opening his eyes and looking at his watch. Okay, well. Darn it. Wait, don't all go. Just one second. Okay, so The Cave is really the world because well, that's the lesson, okay? So please remember to pray for those boys in Thailand, yes, but when they get out of their cave, there's going to be another one, yeah? Because The Cave is the world, do you get that? It's all one big cave and that's why Jesus—okay guys, yeah tear it up, that's right, but you get it? Because what's really outside The Cave is Heaven and that's really where we're going after we get rescued and that's the Jesus part? Everyone gets that? Rachel, explain it back to me.

Do you mean Rachel P. or Rachel W.? someone asked.

Rachel P. is at her dad's this week, someone else said.

Then I mean the only Rachel here today, Pastor Matt said in a sharp voice. Everyone stopped and looked at him.

Rachel Palmers' eyes went wide and darting. Um, that Jesus saves us from The Cave? she said.

Pastor Matt stood and adjusted the brim of his ball cap. Yes, basically, he said. He looked around at the torn and crushed paper. Yes, that's basically it.

Greg Horne lingered as the rest of the group rushed out the double doors. Pastor Matt, I think I have a question, he said. How do we know what's outside The Cave?

Pastor Matt was collecting scraps of brown butcher paper in a garbage bag. It's a, uh, do you do metaphors in school yet? Okay, well, it's one of those. It's pretend to make a point.

So it's not a real cave after we die?

Pastor Matt turned to face him. No, no, no. Life is The Cave, Greg. The world is The Cave. After The Cave is heaven. Because of Easter, remember?

Yeah, Greg Horne said. But I think I still have a question though? Because I think, okay so how do we know? Like, if our whole lives are in The Cave, then how do we know what's outside of it is better or even different? Like, what if after this cave there's just another cave? Or what if it's just... nothing?

Pastor Matt looked into his garbage bag and frowned. He cleared his throat and said, Well, but didn't say anything after. His forehead creased. He stayed like that for a long moment. Eventually, he bent down and returned to picking up the shreds of paper. Greg Horne started to leave

Hey You Assholes

and was almost out the door before Pastor Matt said, Greg hold on a second. When he looked back, Pastor Matt's eyes were shiny again.

Because of the Bible, Pastor Matt said, in a cracked voice. Because that's what it says. There's a verse I'm thinking of in particular. I mean, there's also the, uh, well, I'm forgetting it now for some reason. I mean, I don't know, really. I mean, I'm sorry, I guess. He swallowed. Does that answer your question?

Greg Horne said it did.

Courtney Cousins spilled her Baja Blast and Kenny Lucas ate seven soft tacos before getting sick in the volleyball court and Sharon Hutchinson was pulled aside for a quick chat about being too cliquey and why it's so important to include girls like Kathy Fleming and boys like Gary Medina because they maybe don't have as many friends at their schools, so Mountain Movers becomes a really important part of their week and to keep that in mind, just for next time. And when Pastor Matt was bending down to say this, he took off his ball cap to look Sharon Hutchinson in the eye and when he did, she saw that his hair was different in a way that made her feel sad.

C'mon, Pastor Matt said, quickly putting the hat back on.

They rejoined the rest of the Young Mountain Movers and Pastor Matt stood in the middle of the multipurpose room and waved his hands. This is a good group, he said. Don't you think? I just can't say enough good things about you guys. Don't I say that Mrs. Dernberger? Always how much I love this group?

You do, Mrs. Dernberger said, who had stayed for Taco Bell.

See? I'm serious. Best part of my week, right here, Pastor Matt said.

Other parents began arriving for pick up. They kept their coats on and waited for Pastor Matt to close the meeting in prayer.

Okay gang, let's bow our heads. Heavenly Father, we just come to you tonight in prayer and in fellowship this day, this day you have given us, Lord Jesus, and we thank you God for the opportunity we have to be here and worship you with our relationships with each other. And I just pray for each of these Mountain Movers, Father God, that you may guide them through their own Caves, God, and you deliver them, you *rescue* them because they are your faithful

Hey You Assholes

explorers. Because you are a kind God, a *just* God, and you do not tempt your children, no Jesus, you merely test us, and uh, the Bible says, the Bible says you will not give us more than we can bear, so I guess that means if it's happening then I can bear it, right? You know, I mean, because—

Amen, Pastor Matt, one of the parents said.

Thank you, Pastor Matt, another parent said.

You can beat this thing, Jeremy Howser's dad shouted from the other side of the volleyball court and next to him Robin Dernberger's mom touched the corners of her eyes with a Taco Bell napkin.

Amen, Pastor Matt said, in a voice just above a whisper.

Everyone rumbled Amen in response and the fluorescent lights in the multipurpose room flickered overhead. Coats were zipped, key fobs blorped, and Pastor Matt locked the doors behind us. We sat in the backseats of our warm little cars and drove out into the pale dark, each of us buoyed, at least for the moment, by the unshakeable belief that everyone can be saved.

The Second Time
Vince Broke His Arm

The first time Vince broke his arm, it wasn't my fault. Not either time, actually, but the first one definitely isn't on me. He sued the cop over it, after all.

We were in Orlando for the day, down from Jacksonville because why not and Vince finds some little place on his phone. Says they've got dollar beers. We sit down to order and when the beers arrive they're not normal glasses, not really, they're smaller. I take a sip. Tastes faintly off to me. Can't quite place it.

Vince doesn't mind or doesn't notice. He drains his in one gulp before the waitress leaves and asks for another. I'm pretending not to notice. I can tell he's waiting for me to say something, but I just sip slowly, not a care in the world.

Couple more rounds and he says to the waitress, Just bring me two at a time if you don't wanna keep running back and forth, yeah? Doesn't that make more sense?

What are you doing, I ask him finally.

How can they be making money on these? He is amazed, staring at the beer. Excuse me! This beer should cost at least two dollars! He announces this to the entire dining area. It's just a fantastic deal, he follows up. He gulps two more beers. Just an outstanding deal, he shouts to me.

A cop comes in for take-out and at this point Vince has really got a lather going. Just goofy harmless beer talk, but loud for the lunch crowd. Probably nothing this place hasn't seen before but still. He was asking for it.

Cop says something civil like wanna keep it down, but he's got a look on his face like he drives around looking for shitheads and can't believe his luck. Vince responds with a bunch of attitude. Free country last time I checked, that kind of thing. Not aggressive, not really, but anyone could see the cop wasn't in the mood.

Cop says, Okay buddy, let's go. Time to move along. Vince just sits there, gulps a beer, and crosses his arms. Ends up having to drag Vince out and that's when it happens. Cop's got him on the ground out in the parking lot with his hands behind his back and he's using his knee to pin Vince's wrists down. He's grabbing the zip cuffs when Vince wriggles and the cop loses his balance. Shifts his weight back to the knee that's pinning the wrists and it turns out to be too much. I can hear the snap and that's the first time Vince breaks his arm.

Nothing happens for a second then everything happens all at once. Vince screaming, cop screaming, me screaming.

After the hospital bills and the lawyers, we had more than ten grand leftover. Couple days after the settlement, almost a year after the incident, Vince comes into the kitchen with something in his pocket that I can hear shaking in its plastic container.

He pulls out a big white bottle from his cargo shorts and sets it on the table. I ask him what it is and he says our future and I say, No, really and he says it's pills. It's our future, he says again. And then proceeds to tell me how he's going to sell it for twice what he paid. You're not gonna believe this, he says, but it came out to be exactly how much broken arm money I had left.

I don't even wait for him to finish the sentence before I start crying. I can't help myself because it all starts hitting

Hey You Assholes

me at once. I understand for the first time that I'm poor, that we're poor, that we're poor people, and I don't want this bottle of pills to be my future. I'm trying to say this but it's not coming out right and we start fighting.

The cop didn't break your arm, he says. You could've made me stop drinking but you didn't, he says.

Which is it? I ask. Is the money all yours or do you blame me for letting it happen?

He stares at me. Both, he screams, throwing his hands up as if it was obvious. He's lost in it now, pacing and cursing. Why does everything turn to shit, he shouts.

C'mon man, I say. I'm trying to pull him back, but he's already gone.

Every good thing that happens to me ends up being a bad thing, he says, hitting his head with the flat of his palm.

Vince, stop, I say, but the way he's punching himself means he can't hear me, can't hear anything. You gotta stop, I say.

You gotta stop, he says back at me.

Sometimes, at night, I close my eyes and replay in my head all our aimless boozy hustles. Because even though I ended up leaving, I stayed with him even after Vince broke his arm for the second time. Maybe even stayed because of it.

The second time Vince broke his arm was that night, fighting in the kitchen over the bottle of pills. He broke it so bad the doctor put in pins and screws and everything. You see, all his brain's electricity was demanding his balled fists hit me, but he couldn't. What he did instead was to punch our fridge so hard that it fractured his arm from wrist to shoulder. And how do you not love your friend forever, at least a little, after they do something like that?

A Thin Layer of Frost on Old Decorations

Roland honked outside Heather's parents' house. A few minutes later she came out and waved. He rolled down the window.

You don't want to come in? she said.

Wanna get a good table.

Not even just to say hi? Mom's in there. She wants to see you.

Nah.

Nah?

We're late.

They took the back way. Through the connected neighborhoods. The residential streets.

She looked over at him. Picked something off his sweater. They don't make you like, wear your uniform all the time now?

Nah.

Nah. Is that your new thing? Nah?

He smiled. Yeah.

The pep rally and bonfire were over. The small parking lot was full. Someone with an orange vest directed them to an overflow area.

The band was setting up.

There's Maureen, she said. There's Brett. They'll make room for us.

How's things over there? Brett asked him while Maureen and Heather were in the bathroom.

All right, I guess.

Boring most of the time, I bet.

Well.

No?

Girl got her foot crushed in the weapons elevator last week, Roland said.

Sorry can't hear you.

Said someone got their foot crushed. On the ship.

Ah fuck man.

Stuck in there for a few minutes. Until they figured it out. Screaming god help me. Over and over again.

No shit?

Roland looked away. Nah. Just joking.

The women returned. The band began. In between sets, they said hello to all the people they knew from high school.

You'll be happy to know, Heather said as Roland held her coat for her at the end of the night. You're still the only one I let do this.

Outside was a frozen mist. He shoved his hands into jean pockets. She linked her arm through his. They walked the dark block to his rental car.

Not yet, she said once they got there. I'm not ready yet.

They kept walking. Passed by rows of new storefronts.

This used to be the hardware, Roland said. And this was the, uh. Hmm.

Christian Science Reading Room.

Right.

The nativity scene outside of First Congregational was staged and lit. Roland meandered among the plastic statues, casting big shadows.

When're you going back, he said.

Saturday, she said.

And then what.

And then what what?

You're really going to do it, Roland said, picking up one of the hollow plastic sheep.

Yes, she said. Next year. That's the plan. That's what happens. People get married.

Oh right. He put the plastic sheep under his arm.

Don't take that, she said, even though she was smiling.

Just the one, he said. They've got two others.

You're ridiculous.

They walked back to his car. He put the sheep in the trunk. They held hands on the drive to her parents' place. The windows in the house were dark. He parked on the street.

Here's the thing, Heather said. About you coming in.

It's the last time, Roland said.

That's right.

Inside, a cooking smell filled the living room. A rectangle of soft yellow light cut across the wall from the kitchen.

Heather? a voice whispered.

Yes mom.

Roland with you?

Yes mom.

Better get in here.

Janice stood at the kitchen island in her blousy floral pajamas. Surrounded by bowls of ingredients and spice jars. Flour splotches on her apron. A towel draped over a pie dish. She moved a stack of recipe books and the stepstool out of the way to hug Roland.

Where they have you now?

San Diego.

Oh I see, Janice said, stepping back to take him in. Mister suntan. Mister beach bunny.

Nah.

She was having some wine. Just a little to cook with. She poured two more glasses. She asked about who they saw at the bar, who got fat, who was getting bald.

You know Heather's grandpa was a Navy man, Janice said, uncorking a new bottle of wine. Heather, you know this? That man in uniform! Phew. Seen all these old pictures. No wonder they had so many kids.

Jesus, mom.

Just saying.

Mom, Heather said. How late are you going to stay up?

Stay up? Janice redid her ponytail. Honey, I am up.

I'll get outta your way then, Roland said.

You have somewhere to go today? Your mom's?

Yes.

She hugged him again. Gave his shoulders a little squeeze. It'll be alright, you know, she said, patting his chest.

Roland blinked. I know.

Heather walked him to the door. She grabbed her coat from the bannister.

One more, she said, zipping up.

One more what? It's three in the morning.

One more anything, she said.

* * *

They found an all-night diner. Basement of a building across from the old train station.

I swear, Heather said. I have never seen this place before.

Roland hadn't either. Maybe it's new?

They ordered apple pie to share.

Roland asked the man behind the counter how long they'd been open, but the man pointed out the window.

Look, he said, smiling.

It had just started snowing. They watched it fall for a few minutes without saying anything, the scene outside faintly orange in the streetlights.

We could go back to my mom's, Roland said. Sneak in through the basement.

We could, Heather said.

They walked outside. Heather slid in the slush and spun around on her bootheels.

C'mon, Roland said. I've got an idea.

He drove back to First Congregational and retrieved the hollow plastic sheep from the trunk. They walked hand in hand up the slight rise to the nativity stage. Roland placed the sheep back with the other two.

They stood there watching flurries collect on the nativity. A thin layer of frost on old decorations. It would be the image each would recall for decades to come when someone would mention churches or snow or sheep or love or what it's like to see someone for the last time and not know it.

Listening to Dinosaurs

There came a moment when I was simply too exhausted to go on ignoring them. Riding my bike home from work the hilly way and I had just crested the final rise, that last inside curve on Toro Canyon, I pulled over to the side of the road and paused my little GPS computer.

I was just like, Why not listen to the dinosaurs?

"Thank god," the Velociraptor said, who had been huffing and puffing, running alongside me. The Pterodactyl, swooping low, muttered something about how it was about time.

I was new to California and had been hearing these dinosaurs since getting out of the Navy a year before. When you leave the military, they make you take this civilian transition course. It's not optional. They passed a whole law about it. How to write a cover letter, mock interviews, that kind of thing.

But nothing about if you start seeing dinosaurs. Nothing about what to do if they talk to you.

I propped my bike against the stone wall alongside a gravel driveway that twisted through an avocado orchard. I took a long drink from my water bottle and stretched a hamstring.

"Okay," I said, pointing to the goofy one with these feather horn things. "Let's hear it."

The Carnotaurus (I learned the names later) worriedly scratched at the trunk of a eucalyptus tree with her vestigial forelimbs. "Well," she started. "It's not like we have a specific message or anything…"

She trailed off and poked the Kosmoceratops, an individual I'd come to know as something of a spokesdino.

"We just…" the Kosmoceratops turned toward the ocean. The sunlight caught the thickly chicled skin of his enormous head. "We want to help."

"Help?" I said. "Help how?"

"You know," the Kosmoceratops said. "Like when you're at a crossroads and you need some guiding wisdom."

"Like a guardian angel," I offered.

"I wouldn't say that it's like anything else," the Kosmoceratops said. "We're kind of our own thing."

I asked for an example of the crossroads they're talking about and the Dracorex—this knobby flat-headed bastard—cleared his throat to speak.

"Like at work," he said. "You're not feeling fulfilled, right? Just as an example, I mean. And you're thinking about looking for a new job or whatever and you're weighing your options and you go like, hey, maybe the dinosaurs could help."

I closed my eyes, taking it all in. It's difficult to explain, but at the time, it registered as fitting into a strange kind of logic. All part of my new life as a Californian. I decided to go with the flow, which was something people were always saying out here. That explains it pretty well, actually. I went with the flow.

With the help of the dinosaurs, I made a presentation that garnered widespread praise at work and I also tried a new sex thing with my girlfriend who reported back that pleasure-wise, the experience had been a notch above her expectations. I purchased an electric washer dryer combo over a gas one and took the high road in a situation involving me and the guy my sister married, the result of which was the newly held opinion by my family that I was coming around to be quite the adult.

Hey You Assholes

They weren't a hundred percent on target, though. The dinosaurs, I mean. I lost a medium significant amount of money betting on a football game they swore was going to go a particular way. When it didn't, they claimed that really wasn't how they were meant to help out, which I thought was a convenient framing.

Their range was also quite limited. My father, for instance, was going through something of a late-midlife crisis. They suggested he take out a small business loan and open a premium dog grooming salon.

"That market is very hot right now," the Kosmoceratops reasoned. "It's wide open for entrepreneurship."

"Huh," I said. "Interesting."

As much as someone could get used to that kind of thing, I did. It sounds funny, but in that way, the dinosaurs became part of my routine. Took them for granted, even. Would summon their counsel about where to go for dinner, which slacks go with which shoes, etc.

Then came that business at Rincon beach.

I blew a tire at the bottom of Bates on my way into work is why I was down there. Just past dawn on a gloomy day.

I could see the two women from where I stopped to re-place my tube. One in a wheelchair, the other pushing. They weren't going anywhere though. You could tell by the way they were pointing that they wanted to get to the water's edge but couldn't figure out how with the wheelchair.

The dinosaurs made some grumbling noises like they would have appreciated being brought into this kind of de-cision, but I was already clomping over in my big dorky bi-cycle cleats saying good morning, and waving, like an idiot.

The woman not in the wheelchair introduced herself as Delaney. She was a nurse. She explained how June here used to live in Ventura since back before they built the big highway and she was getting down to her last few days, the hospice doctor said, and Delaney had the idea to get June's old toes wet in the Pacific one last time, that it might help to raise her spirits a bit, which had been quite low lately on account of you-know-what being so close and June being naturally inclined to loneliness and not having the greatest relations with her remaining family, wherever they were.

I looked down at June who gazed vacantly back up at me.

They didn't expect the tide to be out so far, Delaney said. She thought there used to be some kind of pavement path here. That's why they came to this beach specifically.

I have no memory now of offering to help. I just remember doing it. Crouching down and asking if it would be okay and getting the nod in response. Delaney locked the brakes on the wheelchair and June draped an arm around my neck and I picked her up like you'd cradle a baby (she weighed almost nothing and I am kind of muscular) and I followed Delaney's lead down to the ocean where she unfurled a beach towel and where I placed June gently and removed her braided leather huaraches to reveal two of the most beautiful feet I've ever seen.

Jesus, those specimens. They defied everything I knew about women, the world, the basic mechanics of my universe. In some ways, they were more incredible than the dinosaurs.

A few surfers in wetsuits bobbed on their boards near the break. The last fingers of a wave stretched to the edge of our beach towel. "It'll be cold," I warned June, still looking at those marvelous things at the ends of her legs.

We were suddenly breached by the tide and Delaney shrieked and June's toes were more than wet, half her body was soaked through, and I picked her up again out of instinct and Delaney went off chasing the towel and June laughed her phlegmy old lady laugh, enjoying the sight of Delaney, and I, rushing around in a pointless little panic.

Her gray face was so close to mine, so creased and spotted and I thought about those feet of hers, those soft curves around her ankle, the high arch of her sole as smooth as calfskin.

We stayed like that for a moment but Delaney broke in with something about how that was enough excitement for one day and I carried old June back across the sand and returned her somewhat reluctantly to the wheelchair and said goodbye.

I went back to my dinosaurs who had gathered around the bicycle rack.

"I was thinking," I said to the group. "Maybe a few of you could go with her."

"That's not really how this works," the Diplodocus said. She made what I took to be a shrugging motion with her squat leather shoulders.

"I guess I knew that," I said, even though I totally didn't.

What did I know? I mean, really. Not a lot, it was turning out. At least that much was becoming clear.

That morning at Rincon marked a change in my relationship to the dinosaurs. They seemed distracted or disinterested and when I brought it up with them, they accused me of doing the same. Fewer and fewer would muster when I called a session until I stopped doing it so much. Felt like I was bugging them.

Then months later, out of curiosity mostly, I did the thing to make the dinosaurs come and not a single one showed. They were all gone.

I married my girlfriend with whom I tried the new sex thing. She's the only person I've told about the dinosaurs. She asks if I ever see them anymore, whether I still hear their voices from time to time. My honest answer is yes, they're out there, but estranged from me somewhat. As an example, I saw the Kosmoceratops a few weeks ago in the wetlands behind the new housing development they're building in Goleta. I waved but he acted like he didn't notice, which I have to say is very on brand for him.

The truth is they'll always be with me, even if I never see one again. It's the way, after a while, you think of a limp completely separate from the initial wound. In fact, you don't think of it at all.

You're just like, okay, whatever, this is how I move now.

As Planned, We Stopped for Sandwiches

As planned, we stopped for sandwiches in St. Louis on the way to Chicago. We left early enough to get there before noon but by the time we parked, the line for the deli was already wrapped around outside.

"You gotta see these things," Dad said. "You look at it and go, how am I even gonna eat this?"

We had been inching along in line for a few minutes when Hamish said, "Momma hold you?" and was plucked off the ground to straddle her hips.

"This is what I was talking about," Dad said.

"Don't," Mom said.

"He's six, hon."

Mom shifted Hamish up further on her torso and blew her bangs out of her face. "Exactly," she said.

* * *

When it was our turn at the counter, Dad ordered four Aporkalypses with extra Boom Boom sauce on pretzel buns, open face style.

"Wednesday special only sir," the man said. He pointed to the sign in front of the register. "Today's is Mike's Hot and Sloppy."

"You've got to be kidding me," Dad said. "It's on your website."

"As a special," the man said. "On Wednesdays. Try the Mike's Hot and Sloppy. Slow roasted pit beef and cheddar cheese sauce."

"No, I don't think so," Dad said. "No, I think we'll take the pork one. It's called something else now, maybe, but that's what we want. Four of them."

"Hey c'mon, buddy," someone said from farther back in the line.

"The Muffuletta is also pretty popular," the worker said.

"It's just that we came for it specifically," Dad said. "I brought my whole family. I mean, I grew up around here. Not here exactly, not this neighborhood. But I used to come here all the time. Marty will remember me, if he's still around."

"We run outta the pork every week, sir," the man said. "Even if it was Wednesday, there's no guarantee."

"Hey asshole," a different someone said from back in the line.

Dad looked at me and I shrugged. "What a total disaster," Dad said and ordered four Mike's Hot and Sloppies.

The sandwiches came wrapped in thick white paper and we sat on the back patio in wobbly chairs to eat them.

"Maybe it wouldn't have been as good as I remember it," Dad said between bites. "Maybe it's a good thing in a way."

Mom got up to get more napkins and when she was gone, Dad turned to me and said, "I'm doing this because you can handle it. Okay?" and I said okay.

She came back with wet wipes and boxes for leftovers and we did our best with the sandwiches but they were true to their name and eventually she said that we had better get on the road if we wanted to miss Chicago traffic. He told her to sit down for a sec.

"I've made a decision," Dad said. "I'm not going to Chicago." He swigged the last of his grape soda.

"You're not," she said.

Hamish raised his hand. "Yes Hamish," Dad said.

"Then where will you get the surgery?"

"That's a good question, buddy. I'm not going to get the surgery."

"Rich, seriously," Mom said.

"It's my decision, Jo. In the end, I mean, it's mine to make."

"I don't even know what to say," she said.

"It's a trial," he said. "It's an experiment. It's not a miracle. Best case scenario? What do I get? More bad days? I'd rather have fewer good days. With you all." He reached for her but she crossed her arms. "I talked to Brendan about it already. He understands, dontcha bud?"

"Dad," I said.

"Anyway this is not a discussion. It's a nice day and we just had lunch and now we're gonna drive back home. I don't wanna talk about it anymore. Okay?"

The man who took our order came over to our table with a doggie bag. "Hey sir, so I remembered there was some smoked shoulder left over from a catering order. I told the boys in the kitchen you were a former local and they did the rest. So. Here ya go. On the house. Okay, no problem sir."

After he left, Dad turned to Mom, who was crying, and said, "Did you do this?"

"Well, I told them why we're going to Chicago, if that's what you're asking," she said. "Or why we were going anyway."

"Jo," he said standing up. "We can still go."

"No, we don't have to." Mom brushed the crumbs from her blouse. "You're right. It's your decision. I don't know what I was thinking. Of course we don't have to go."

He looked at the bag. "But if I want to," he said.

Mom called to Hamish, who was pulling ivy down from a fence. She turned back to Dad. "But you don't," she said.

Dad didn't say anything. He opened the white paper bag, already spotted with pork grease and stuck his face in, breathing deeply. He opened his eyes and closed the bag.

"No," he said finally. "I really don't."

Hey You Assholes

Terminal Leave

Slater's got the PTSD.

She says it just like that.

Not from combat, though. She's a pay clerk after all. It's from this other thing that happened to her. She's not saying what. At least not to us. And by us I mean the people who muster together in the morning at base admin while the Navy sorts out our situation. You know—the fuck ups, the fat bodies, the fakers.

And speaking of fakers, Rutherford says Slater's story is just that.

A story.

A hustle.

A get-out-of-uniform-no-questions-asked card.

"Not a judgment, just an observation," says Rutherford.

Keep in mind that Rutherford doesn't have much room to talk. She's fighting an ADSEP charge for popping on a piss test. At a party and got a headache and someone gave her a pill she thought was whatever but turned out to be something else. Ecstasy, the test said.

"Thing is," Rutherford says. "It did help my headache go away."

Ha ha.

Rutherford's got jokes.

She knows it doesn't look good. She's just waiting on the official word.

It's a shame too because Rutherford, ecstasy incident notwithstanding, is a pretty squared away petty officer. Hard-charger, even. Squadron sailor of the year. Sikorsky maintenance man of the quarter. A green shirt on back-to-back deployments. Launched jets from the middle of the Arabian sea and around the horn of Africa and somewhere in the Somali Basin.

More impressive considering she's so tiny.

Five feet if she's lucky.

Drowns in the smallest uniform they can issue her.

Sitting shotgun in the duty van next to me, her blue camo sleeves swallow her little hands.

Why we've got the duty van is because we've got appointments.

Appointments! we tell Chief.

Medical appointments. Legal appointments. No one has more appointments than me and Rutherford.

But really we just use the duty van to fuck off.

If someone thought to check, we'd probably be in some shit. But it's not like Rutherford can get into more trouble. And me? I simply have stopped caring.

Anyway, I like our little conspiracy. Also I'm kind of in love with her.

Or I am until the ADSEP board comes back with their decision. Slater breaks the news to me. I'm looking for Rutherford but Slater says I just missed her.

Bad conduct discharge. BCD.

Winner, winner, big chicken dinner.

"Damn," I say.

"Damn is right," says Slater. She points at the duty van keys in my hand. "Where ya goin?"

* * *

We are going to Bellingham. Me and Slater. No real reason.

"What's your story," Slater asks, sitting shotgun in the duty van.

I say I don't have one.

"Everyone has a story."

"Not me, I guess."

We stop for coffee at this roadside kiosk where the baristas wear thong bikinis.

"Oh so you're a pig," Slater says.

She gets a muffin. Eats it in pinches over the next hour.

It's raining when we get to Bellingham. This constant misty drizzle.

I ask Slater what she wants to do. She asks me what I usually do.

"This is pretty much it," I say.

We drive until we see a sign for the Canadian border. We turn around.

"Okay then," Slater says after a long stretch of silence. "Make one up. A story. Like about who you are and stuff."

"I told you. I don't really have one."

"That's why you gotta make one up."

Fuck *off*, I want to say.

"Like you did?" I say instead.

"Like I did what?"

"Whatever you told the doctors to make them think you have the PTSD," I say. "Now *that's* a story I'd like to hear."

"I do have the PTSD," Slater says. "I mean, really. I have it. I have paperwork. I have the fucking PTSD!"

"Rutherford didn't think so," I say.

Slater does a voice. "*Rutherford says, Rutherford says,*" even though this is the first I'm bringing her up.

"It's just that you always seemed fine to me," I say. "In fact, this is the most worked up I've ever seen you."

"Well, I don't have to tell you anything," Slater says. "It's the law."

"Medical conditions, right."

Traffic is backed up crossing the bridge to Whidbey. We slow to a crawl and then stop completely. Slater rolls down the window and cranes her neck out.

"Something happened," she reports back.

I put the duty van in park. We wait. Three songs and a commercial break go by on the radio.

"Okay fine then," Slater says. "Okay, I'll tell you. Do you still wanna know?"

I make a gesture like I'm-all-ears, baby.

"I do have a medical condition. But you're right. It's not PTSD." She covers her face with her hands and takes a deep breath. "I have Down syndrome," she says.

We inch forward in traffic. Barely.

"Fuck off, please," I say.

"No really," Slater says, lifting her face and smiling. "I'm a retard." She droops her eyelids and sticks her tongue out.

Ha ha.

Slater's got jokes.

"That's not funny," I say.

"Then why are you laughing?" Slater asks, continuing the impression. She adds some noises.

"I'm not," I say, even though I am a little.

"See?" Slater says. "Aren't I better than little old Rutherford?"

"No comment," I say.

She changes the radio station. "What are you getting out for anyway? Huh? What's so wrong with you?"

Since leaving Bellingham, the day has cleared. A group of cyclists ride past us on the shoulder. "Nothing's wrong with me. I'm not getting out. I've got hard orders to base admin."

"Really? I thought it was just civilian contract people in the enlisted billets there."

Fuck it, I think.

"Yeah, they phased out active duty about a year ago." I glance over at her from behind my sunglasses. "I was on staff when it happened. Everyone was supposed to get new orders, but there was some kind of mix up in Millington. My detailer told me I was going to a flag assignment in Oceana, but when I got my official orders, it said to depart from NAS Whidbey Island to permanently change duty station to… NAS Whidbey Island."

"Ha," Slater says. "Classic."

"Yeah, but I didn't point it out to the travel clerk or anything," I say.

"It's just a typo, man."

"No, they're official orders," I say. "Got a big stamp on them that says so."

"Yeah, but…" Slater trails off, thinking. "I mean—"

"Really, I thought someone would catch it. But no one did. Everyone was going on leave so I did too. Took like 30 days. Came back and the rest of my shop had already detached. My entire chain of command. That's when I saw the group of the TAD folks mustering. I went over to see if I knew anyone. Chief asked if there was anyone whose name he didn't call. I didn't really think about it. I just raised my hand."

"Damn. And you're still getting paid? This was how long ago?" Slater asks.

"A year. Almost a year."

She shakes her head. "But like, someone's gotta figure it out though, right? On some spreadsheet somewhere? Budgets and manning and all that? Someone is gonna be short one asshole."

"That's what I'm saying. I thought so too. And yet here I am."

"Jesus. I mean…" She trails off again, looking out the window. "I mean, what're you gonna *do*? Just keep milking it? I mean, what's your *plan*?"

I gesture to the duty van, the traffic jam, the forest of Washington state surrounding us. "You're looking at it." I say.

* * *

Hey You Assholes

The traffic eventually clears and we stop at a gas station after crossing the bridge back to the island. Slater hops out to use the bathroom. At the spot next to ours, a kid sitting in the backseat of a sedan watches me pump gas through an open window.

He points at me. I wave hello.

A man gets out of the sedan and approaches. He gestures to the kid. "He wants to see your uniform up close," he says. "That okay?"

I say of course it is. I give the kid a high five. Show him all my Velcro pockets.

"You can ask him now," the man says to the kid.

"What's your job in the Army?"

"To him, not to me," the man says.

"What's your job in the Army?"

"The Navy, actually," I say to the kid.

"See?" the man says. "See how they have different uniforms?"

"Well, I'm gonna be an Army man," the kid says.

Slater comes out of the convenience store and walks over to us.

"Meet a future soldier," I say to her.

The man thanks us for our service. We're almost about to leave when I hear a knock on my window. The man again.

"This is gonna sound—well, I just wanted to ask. No stupid questions, right?" He clears his throat into his fist. "He can't do it, can he? Join? None of the branches, right? He wouldn't be allowed?"

I look over at Slater. She doesn't know what to say either.

"I know, I know. I'm pretty sure he can't. But here's my question, though okay? You know how they have the Special Olympics? Well, have you ever heard of something like that? Like, the military version?"

He stares right at me. I could tell him anything, but he already knows. I say I'm sorry, but I haven't heard of anything like that before.

I start to say something else but he cuts me off. "Yeah okay. Damn. Stupid, I know." He claps his hand against the duty van door. "All right then."

Slater and I don't talk much the rest of the way back.

It's getting dark and we're a couple miles from base when Slater starts giggling quietly to herself.

Takes me a little to realize she's crying.

Says she doesn't really have the PTSD. Says she made the whole thing up.

Doesn't know why. Doesn't have a plan. Just needs a fresh start. Doesn't care where.

Says she thought her life would be different. Can't say exactly how. Says she imagined things would happen in a way that made sense, but they didn't. Instead nothing made sense. Instead everything felt like an accident, like random, like what was she doing? Like what the hell, you know?

Says she's sorry for crying, sorry for all the drama.

She's still going when I get this crazy feeling. Dark lightning, I don't know. Like a big happy wolf. That's the best way I can describe it. Like a big happy and hungry cartoon wolf. Like if I could do anything, what would I do?

Maybe keep driving.

Just keep going.

No plans. No uniforms.

A little bit of something after so much nothing.

Stupid, I know.

"Hey that was the gate, I think," Slater says next to me.

"Was it now," I say, and press my boot down hard on the accelerator.

The World's Biggest Moron Stops Laughing

I find the proof I hoped I wouldn't while my mom is telling me how she disapproves of my dad's new hobby, which is growing marijuana in the basement of the house I grew up in, the one they still live in, a two-story craftsman, a century home with a brass plaque to prove it, three red states and a time zone away.

In one hand I am holding my phone to my ear and in my other I am holding Molly's phone, who is in the shower and who is my wife and whose birthday is 09-17-84, which is her passcode, which I type in, and what I see in her messages opens a cavern in my crotch, a great cosmic fissure starting at my loins and splitting through my skull and the words I read are familiar and foreign at the same time.

The last thing my wife typed and sent. *I never thought I'd love sucking cock*, it reads. *But I do now.*

Then a crazy face.

Then an upside down smiley face.

"He calls it the big tree, but it's really all these little ones. 'Gotta go see about my big tree.' Like it's a farm chore!" my mom says in my ear.

Molly calls my penis my Wing Wang, my Thing Ding, my Little Man, my Downstairs Guy. Always has. Even in our hot days, our way back days. Ours is a cockless marriage.

"It's drugs, okay? And then he's always after me to try it, which, yeah right mister."

I hear the water from Molly's shower rushing through the pipes in the walls of the house we bought together. That was seven years ago. Cash was cheap. The deal we got beggared belief. Everyone was jealous. I look down at her phone again.

But I do now.

"I mean, it'd be one thing if it was outside. At least he'd be getting some fresh air. But he has this tent in the basement. All these lights too. You know what he's like, it's a whole operation. I'm thinking, is this a drug den? I mean officially?"

I'm poking around the wreckage of my insides to see what remains and at the dawn of knowing an angry fire burned hot, but now the only feeling left is shame and filth and ache and ashes because I've known without evidence for months and did nothing, swatted the idea away from my face where all summer it buzzed in angry circles and this, this moment while she's still in the shower is my shriveled dick chickens coming home to roost.

"He has cancer, mom," I tell her.

But what I'm really thinking about is my wife's wet, naked body with someone who isn't me. My Thing Ding curiously stirs. Fuck you, I say to it. You don't know what the fuck you're talking about.

"Had," she says. "He had cancer and that was years ago. We're down to an annual visit to Dr. Khan and now he needs this for pain management? You can't see me, but I'm doing those finger quotes."

I try to picture Molly saying the words I'm reading in her messages, but I can only see her mouth moving and no sound. *Love sucking cock*, she says on a muted loop in my head. Upstairs, the shower water shuts off. I hear her step out of the bathtub and creak across the floor.

"When you all visit for Christmas, you'll see," my mom is saying. "Just how ridiculous he's being. That's why I'm telling you. I need an ally. Your sisters don't know and I don't want them to. I mean, the whole house just reeks. It's like I'm married to Rob Marley!"

Upside down smiley face. What does that mean, I asked Molly when we first got engaged. She said it meant that she was so in love that her body ceased to be governed by gravity.

"I think with you and me and Molly it will really seem like a unified front. Have you seen these interventions? They do a whole show about it and that's what I have in mind."

My mom saying Molly's name strikes me as singularly funny for some reason. In my lap, Molly's phone makes a pinging noise. Incoming message from the person who's cock she loves sucking.

Better late than never, it says. Then a winky face. Then a tongue.

Then a heart.

Then Molly comes down the stairs in a towel and goes to the outlet where she left her phone charging but it's not there. She looks up to see me holding one phone to my ear and holding her phone in my lap. I have a thought that if we'd had a son, this is how he'd look at me when I'd catch him jerking off. She puts her face in her hands and yells, Oh god. The towel falls down. Her pale tits make two sad eyes above the smiling crease of her navel. I start laughing. I can't help it.

"Please," my mom says, exhausted. "Tell me what is so hilarious about your father being helplessly addicted to drugs."

Molly is wailing at me to give her the phone but all I can do is laugh. My eyes mist and my body shakes. I am powerless to stop it. What's happening inside me is chemical. It has breached the threshold. The Coke bottle of infidelity and the Mentos of my mom and the insane burping giggles bursting forward.

It all starts running together. My dad in the basement sucking cock, my wife as the angel on a Christmas tree, my mom smoking marijuana upside down in the shower. If I could tell them, they'd laugh too but when I open my mouth what comes out instead is the voice of the world's biggest moron and when he finally stops laughing, the only thing he can say is, I'm sorry, I'm sorry, I'm sorry, I'm sorry.

Hey You Assholes

Be Gentle

"Think about it like this," I tell her. "We call it computer class but it's not really a class. Just like I work at the school but am not really a teacher." She stares at me blankly. "Just like even though these are pictures of naked women, it's not pornography. This is art." She gives me no indication that I'm breaking through. She called me over claiming the boy sitting next to her was looking at porn. I can't remember the girl's name, only that in our few exchanges her frequency registered as someone who does school plays.

The websites we let the students visit are pretty limited so what I found on the screen of the computer terminal next to her were high quality photos of ancient nude sculptures taken in a museum. Who I found looking at them was a fat kid with glasses wearing a shirt with a dragon graphic wrapped all the way around.

"Is this for a project?" I ask him.

"Um," he says.

"Look at something else, please."

"I like them," he says. "Like white chocolate." He licks the screen. It makes a staticky sound.

The girl stands up. "I'm going to tell Ms. Vaughn." She stands in front of my desk with her arms crossed as I write her a pass. Ms. Vaughn is the Vice Principal and it's whose office I am sitting in before I leave for the day. I am there at the request of a note that came by student courier. It arrived shortly after the girl went to tattle on the boy, whose name I discovered was EJ.

Ms. Vaughn is smiling at me with her mouth closed from across her desk. I am wondering if I should call her by her first name and whether her first name is Tracy or Trudy. She asks me if I want a bottle of water and I say no and she tells me not to be nervous.

"I want to let you know this is not one of those yell-at-the-new-guy things," she starts. "I think this is much more of a I-want-to-help-you-succeed-here kind of thing." Ms. Vaughn goes on to explain that this incident in the computer lab was not the first, but rather the most recent in a long series of EJ's behavior that could only be described as disturbing.

"Of course you know about the yawning." I shake my head. "Every time someone yawned, he would stick his hand in their mouth. This was in middle school. He was told to stop and he wouldn't. He *couldn't*. He wasn't doing it to be funny. He was doing it because it *upset* people. Because it was a *violating* behavior. He scared people. Oh, and the algebra book. He ate an entire algebra workbook. This was last year, his freshman year. Every day, he'd tear out two pages and eat them. Chew, swallow, the whole deal. Mrs. Flagler—she left, got pregnant—sometimes she'd send him to me and sometimes she'd just try to ignore him. End of the semester, he'd eaten every single page."

"That's pretty unusual."

"Mr. Culberson, yes that's very unusual. I'm starting to see why Mary Ann came to me. I don't think you understand how much EJ bothers the other students. How disturbing this kind of thing is to the other students who are here to learn. We owe it to the ones who are serious about their future to maintain an environment—yes, even in computer class—where they can do that."

"Ms. Vaughn—"

"Safety, Mr. Culberson. You are not an educator. I respect your experience, being what it is, but what it is not is a degree in education. You are a supervisor. You are here to make sure no one gets hurt. You are here to make sure everyone uses the computers in a responsible way." She narrows her eyes. "Safety, James."

"I understand."

"You know, I remember you from when you went here. People don't think I remember them, but I'm good with faces and I remember you. I also know you served this country and that's a big part of why you're here too. I want this to be a place for people like you." She stood up from behind her desk and knocked her fist against the wall behind her. "But this is the real world. And they're just kids. So the next time you see boobs on a computer screen, marble or not, I want detention. And the next time EJ acts out, I want to hear from you, not a student. Okay?" She walks around the desk and opens the door for me.

"Thank you, Tracy," I say, walking out the door.

"Oh, you're going to do great here. You'll get the hang of it," she says. "You're a natural." And then, after I'm almost to the end of the hall, she leans out her door and through cupped hands stage-whispers, "It's Trudy, by the way."

* * *

I have EJ next week on a different day at a slightly different time. There's some kind of elaborate rotation at the school and they group the kids together in pods and each one is named after an animal. EJ and Mary Ann are Otters. It's halfway through the Otter hour when Mary Ann comes to my desk.

"Mr. Culberson, EJ is bothering me." I ask her what he's doing because from where I'm sitting it didn't look like he was doing anything except for looking up photos of dinosaurs and drawing them in his notebook. I've been extra diligent in checking his screen.

"Mr. Culberson, he keeps poking me with his finger and saying that he's putting his eggs in me."

I go over to EJ's workstation. "Don't touch other students," I say to him. He looks up at me, eyes squished in his fat face and says okay.

Mary Ann comes back a few minutes later. "Mr. Culberson, EJ said he's putting eggs in me *with his mind*."

I write EJ a pass to Ms. Vaughn's office and phone down to let her know he's on his way. Mary Ann goes back to her chair, crosses her legs at the ankles, rests her chin on the platform made from her laced fingers and propped elbows, and returns to reading the Wikipedia entry for dressage.

"EJ," I say before he leaves the classroom. "Next class, come sit by me." He blinks his eyes. "But no weird shit, okay?"

The curse makes him grin. He says, "Okay, Mr. Culberson."

I wish I could say that fixed him, that EJ was never disturbing again, but of course he kept doing weird shit. Sharpening his pencils and putting them between his fingers like Wolverine and then running at other kids saying, "Make way, mortals!" I field-tested my admonitions until I landed on the most effective, which was a half-bored but stern sounding, "Knock it off, EJ."

It also didn't stop him from bothering students in other classes. Claiming to be a monkeyboy and only answering to the name Monkey Boy. That kind of thing. But sitting next to me, using my computer when it was the Otters turn for computer class kept him out of the way and that resembled a kind of understanding. An armistice.

Hey You Assholes

* * *

It's a few weeks later when I'm arriving at school that I see EJ standing by the field near the teacher's parking lot. He's just standing there motionless by a patch of flowers with his arms outstretched, palms upward. I start walking over to him and when I get close enough, I can see the bees. A swarm of them, buzzing around EJ, whose eyes are closed and either doesn't see or hear me or is pretending like he can't. The bees land on him and fly off, but EJ doesn't flinch. His fleshy arms are pale and unstung. I watch until he breaks his stillness, until he bends over and plucks a flower from the ground. He's doing something I can't see with it and I turn around to head inside before he knows I was there.

I have the Otters first period that day and EJ comes in early because he always comes in early. He takes his seat, which is my seat, in front of the computer to log on and I tell him what I saw with the bees.

"Oh that," he says. He types something on the keyboard and brings up the Wikipedia page for bees. He scrolls down and points a pudgy finger at the screen. "It says you have to be gentle."

"And they don't sting you?"

"No way," he says and scoops his hand into the breast pocket of the hot air balloon-sized bowling shirt he's wearing and brings out a flower bloom with its petals closed up. EJ pinches one petal back and a fuzzy bee steps out onto his palm. The bee shakes some pollen off. It starts walking the length of EJ's hand and then onto the other one and then back again and then back into the flower, which EJ puts in his shirt pocket. I ask what he's going to do with it and he shrugs.

"Let it go, I guess," he says.

"That's a special thing, EJ. Do you know that?" Pink blooms on his cheeks.

"Mr. Culberson," he says. "Do you know that the other teachers don't like me?" He looks down. I don't know what to say and so I don't say anything. The first bell rings in the silence.

"I think you're probably right about that," I say, finally.

"But you like me, though?" he asks, looking up.

Later this hour, he'll pick his nose and wipe it on Mary Ann and get sent to Ms. Vaughn's again. The summer before his senior year he'll get a growth spurt and be recruited to play offensive tackle where he'll help the team make the playoffs for the first time since I was in high school. EJ's helmet will come off during a play but he'll spear the runner anyway, gashing his head open. He'll return to the bench, blood streaming down into his smiling face, the other boy unconscious, and that will be what punches his ticket. Charges will be filed and then dropped, but EJ will still get expelled. Later he'll get his GED and join the Marines and come back fucked up so when I see him next, it's when I'm dropping off my car at a Jiffy Lube. He won't recognize me and I won't say anything, just a polite thank you. I'll see what's left of him is the EJ who put a boy in the hospital in that football game and what's gone is the part of him that could pet a bumblebee.

"I don't know, EJ," I tell him. The rest of the Otters start arriving and chatter blooms in pockets of the classroom as they sit down. The soft electric burning rises in my nose as the machines turn on. "I'm not a teacher."

The Quest
For Blaine

Everyone wants to hear the horror stories. When they ask, that's what they're asking about. Like the time after your second deployment when your folks threw you a homecoming. And one of your dad's work friends says, What the hell did you even do over there anyway? And the way he says it, you can tell he's joking a little, but lately it's the little things that have been setting you off and you say, Well, we tried to help and he says, How did that work out? and you say, Well, they all died and he says, What are you talking about? and you say, Everyone died. The SEAL too. He got stabbed in the neck, you say. And now everyone is looking at you, but you're just getting started.

Stabbed in the neck, you say, louder. But that happened later. You want to know what happened first. They were missionaries, right? On this yacht in the Somali basin. And the pirates came, took it over. It's a business there, you know. And they say they want money or they're gonna kill the Christians and dump the bibles into the ocean or whatever.

And now your parents are kind of looking at each other and your dad's work friend steps closer. He starts saying something, but you cut him off.

Well, we tried to help, you say. But they all died and the SEAL got stabbed in the neck. He didn't die right away. He died eventually, you say. They flew his remains off the ship a few days later. Everyone went up to the flight deck. It was kind of a ceremony, you explain.

You show him on his neck where the stab happened. Right here, you say, sawing your hand where his neck meets his shoulder. To the hilt.

That part you make up, because who could know that except for a few people and you weren't one of those people. But it feels true to you in the moment and now everyone's coming over to where you're shouting and someone takes the wine glass out of your hand and you tell everyone you're fine.

You hear someone start crying and you think it's your mom so you yell at her to stop but then you realize it's you,

you're the one who started crying. Jesus, I'm sorry, you say. Goddamnit, you say, closing your eyes to stop from crying. It doesn't help. They leak like they're broken.

They gave everyone medals, you say. I guess that's what bothers me.

Your former fiancée's parents are there. Or were. At some point during this—let's call it an episode—they leave. You imagine the story they'll tell her and you picture her on the other end of the phone, laying in bed alone. You imagine her afterwards, drinking the cool blue water on her nightstand, totally unburdened by the life she would have had with you.

And you, you tragic weirdo, are stuck forever in that living room. You are doomed to tell a story that never ends.

What did you do over there? your dad's new work friend asks.

Well, we tried to help, you say.

Master Guns

I didn't like Master Guns. Not one bit. For one thing, his appointment with Chaps was at 10am, but he always came a few minutes early to bother me.

"Here he is," he'd say, leaning against my desk. "The world's biggest Nancy Pelosi fan."

"I don't know who that is," I'd tell him for the thousandth time, but eventually I learned that she was the Speaker of the House of Representatives until the 2010 midterm elections when she was replaced by John Boehner.

Master Guns did not love John Boehner, but he hated Nancy Pelosi.

"I hate Nancy Pelosi," he'd say. Then, upon glancing at the Oswald Chambers daily meditation calendar Chaps had put next to the coffee machine, "Nancy Pelosi," he'd grumble. "She's the least of my problems."

I didn't like Master Guns, but he was right about that.

* * *

In truth, Master Guns had many problems and that's why he had a standing appointment with Chaps. From my desk outside his office I could hear Master Guns' side of the conversation because he shouted almost everything. They usually began each of their sessions with some kind of debate about Obama or the Tea Party which quickly fell away to reveal the problems Master Guns was really there to talk about.

"She's leaving me, Chaps!" He meant his wife. I had learned the saga of Master Guns and his wife that winter, during my first deployment sailing across the Atlantic ocean in a slate gray floating city that carried 5,000 of my best friends from Norfolk harbor to the Northern Arabian Sea.

The USS Enterprise fought in Vietnam fifty years ago and now it was fighting another war. This time, I was on it. So was Master Guns.

"Oh she's a bitch, all right, Chaps!" He meant his wife again. And this was another thing I didn't like about Master

Hey You Assholes

Guns. From what I could piece together, his wife was indeed leaving him, but that wasn't what made her a bitch. What made her a bitch was that when he left for deployment, she discovered some emails which indicated that an Xbox that went missing from the wardroom a year ago had actually been stolen by Master Guns and sold on Craigslist. Among the Xbox emails were other messages Master Guns had sent to a woman in Reno, with whom he was having an affair. She was a bitch because she sent all of this evidence to the squadron commander, who opened an investigation.

"She's just trying to get back at me! She's destroying my career!"

And then Master Guns would sob because at the age of 42, he had ascended to the highest rank an enlisted man could attain in the Marine Corps and he had married a woman who was now sitting alone in his gaudy Florida mansion and whose sole mission was to dissemble her husband's sanity, one email to his commander at a time.

And there was nothing he could do about it.

* * *

I did not feel sorry for Master Guns, mainly because I was too busy feeling sorry for myself. It was my first deployment and the feelings of adventure I thought I would have did not materialize. Instead, I drifted around the ship like a ghost, see-through and only half there.

If I told you that every sailor was heartbroken in their own special way, would you believe me? Because they are. The day before I left for Norfolk, I spent the day drinking beer with a girl who—more than anything and for reasons beyond my understanding—wanted to be my girlfriend. She told me so at a sushi restaurant in a strip mall where she had invited me to say goodbye.

"I want to be your girlfriend," she said. "I want to miss you when you're gone."

"You will," I said. "I don't know what you want from me."

"Yes you do," she said.

"I promise you," I said slowly. "I have no idea what you want."

She turned away from me and frowned. She taught fourth grade somewhere in the swamp and the kids in her classes made fun of her car. She told me that the night we met.

"What kind of car do you drive?" I asked her then.

"It's a Kia," she said demurely.

"Why would they make fun of your car?" I asked.

"I'm not sure," and she smiled in a way that made me feel like she did know, but I would have to earn the answer from her. I never did.

After sushi, we went back to my apartment and sat on my bed. She looked glum and wasn't hiding it. I had an idea.

"Wait right here," I told her. I went into my closet and pulled out a brand-new leather jacket, still in the box that it came in. I bought it the year before as a gift for my fiancée, which was back when I still had a fiancée. Now I just had the jacket.

"I got this for you," I lied.

She gasped. "It's beautiful!" She tried it on. I could see that it was too big for her, but if she noticed, she didn't care. "It's beautiful," she said again, her eyes wet and shiny.

"I got it for you," I repeated. I said it because I wanted it to be true, because the jacket was supposed to belong to the person I was going to marry, but instead it sat in my closet for a year, fucking with me. Now I was giving it away to make another girl feel better, but also because I thought it would make me feel better. It worked on her but not on me. I didn't feel anything. In the hours after she left, I felt worse.

Later she texted me a photo of her wearing the jacket. She had pushed up the sleeves like Miami Vice so it would fit her short arms. In one hand, she held the note I had written to my fiancée. It was a note I had forgotten was still in the inside pocket. Her other hand was giving me the middle finger.

I didn't feel sorry for Master Guns, but I also wasn't in a place to judge him.

* * *

In the Navy, you don't always do the job you sign up to do. It's almost a running joke.

There was a guy who worked in the Chief's Mess washing dishes and he would sneak me fresh fruit and yogurts in exchange for saved seats during Chaps' Sunday services in the hangar bay. I would go see him in a compartment we called the Deep Sink. He wore thick rubber gloves to his elbows and a heavy synthetic apron, black and flecked with bits of old food. He told me that he was a trained Navy paralegal, but I couldn't believe it. It must be a punishment, I thought. The Deep Sink was a terrible assignment—twelve hours on your feet, blasting the stinking remains of our meals into oblivion.

One day I asked him if he was down there because he got in trouble. He smiled and said, "Nope. Just lucky."

We called him the Zen Master.

So the job you sign up to do isn't always the job you end up doing. I was supposed to be an avionics expert but I did not feel like an expert of anything. Every squadron has to provide support personnel to the ship during deployment. The Zen Master went to the Deep Sink. I was detailed to Chaps.

* * *

Chaps was the Chaplain for the air wing and his official title was Lieutenant Doug Russell, but everyone called him Chaps. He wore a flight suit and his shoulder patch was a Methodist cross, glowing white beams and licks of red flame. He had requested support personnel and I was that support, but he didn't seem to have much for me to do. My daily duties were as follows:

Post the schedule.

Make the coffee.

Flip the Oswald Chambers calendar to the next day.

Standby.

He led a weekly Bible study and he would sometimes test out his lessons on me. Mostly, he was like every other religious person in the Navy—well-meaning and inscrutable.

One day, he instructed me to watch *Anger Management*, which at the time had been out for over seven years. It's a movie with Adam Sandler and Jack Nicholson and Chaps told me to take notes.

That afternoon, I sat cross-legged in the enlisted berthing with a pad of paper and a pen, watching the movie intently. I did not know what I was supposed to be looking for. I realized halfway through that I hadn't taken a single note. During the next scene, Jack Nicholson screamed at Adam Sandler and he screamed back at him. I wrote down, "Old Testament?"

I worried for a week that Chaps was planning to quiz me about the movie, but he never brought it up again. Years later I would think I saw him on a MILAIR flight from the Seychelles to Naples and I would panic for a moment, thinking he would bring up *Anger Management* and I would have nothing to say. I won't know what to make of the relief I felt when I saw it wasn't him.

* * *

Master Guns was the first person I met after getting detailed to Chaps. He burst through the door, all five feet and three inches of him, looking like he owned the place, which is pretty typical for senior enlisted Marines.

Master Guns is short for Master Gunnery Sergeant, which is the same rank as Sergeant Major, but also very different. The difference is that Sergeant Majors are in charge. They are often legendary and scary motherfuckers. Master Gunnery Sergeants, however, are supposed to be technical people. Some lean into the role as a subject matter expert, which is some mix of consultant and oracle. Others feel like not being chosen for command is an insult and spend the rest of their careers wallowing in the wake of the slight. It did not take me long to figure out which Master Guns was.

"Who the fuck are you?" he asked me, narrowing his eyes.

"I'm helping Chaps. I'm new." I said.

"Yeah, you're new all right," he said. "Who'd you vote for?"

"I, uh, Obama."

"Not for president, shipmate. The midterms. The midterms!"

"I don't—" I started and was saved when Chaps came out of his office.

"Paul," Chaps said. "C'mon in."

Master Guns walked past my desk towards Chaps. "We'll pick this up later, shipmate."

I heard him inside. "Where do they find these guys?" he asked Chaps.

"Oh he's not so bad," Chaps replied.

I didn't like Master Guns. Not one bit.

* * *

That was the deployment where Lieutenant Donnelly implemented his Eight-On-Eight-Off protocol for the aircrewman. Usually, everyone on the ship worked in twelve-hour shifts. There is a night crew and a day crew. Lieutenant Donnelly wanted to try rotating eight-hour shifts. You'd be on for eight hours, then off for eight hours, then back on again. The idea was that it would prevent burnout and keep everyone sharp, fit, and rested.

What happened is that people went crazy.

I don't mean that people became overworked and cranky. I mean that the aircrew started to see impossible things.

I found out about it when I went to the squadron briefing room to watch *Braveheart* with Ruben. There was a big TV in there and if there were no night flight operations, the officers let the enlisted sailor on watch pick a movie to put on the projector. Ruben was the aircrewman on the desk that night and I went down because he always put on *Braveheart*.

I walked into the briefing room to see Ruben pleading with Lieutenant Donnelly.

"C'mon, sir," Ruben begged. "Just the battle scenes."

"Absolutely not. I cannot watch this movie again."

"It's the only DVD I have," Ruben admitted.

"Then what's this?" Lieutenant Donnelly picked up a DVD near Ruben's laptop.

"That's not mine," Ruben said.

"That is, uh," I said, trying to be helpful. "That looks like disc two of *Sopranos* season four."

"Great! Yes! That's what we're watching!" Lieutenant Donnelly grabbed the DVD, put it in the tray, and mushed it into the player. Then he spun on his heel and left.

"If he was going to leave, then why would he care what we watched?" I asked Ruben.

"It's the aliens," Ruben said dryly. "Everyone is worked up over the aliens."

And then he told me about how the crews for the last few nights of patrols had reported seeing something strange, something fast. The Captain blamed Lieutenant Donnelly's Eight-On-Eight-Off protocol. He said it was causing sleep deprivation and that's why the aircrew would come back from patrols with mission reports where everyone would see something unexplainable, but would be unable to say exactly what they saw.

"So no more eight-hour shifts?" I asked him. Ruben smiled.

"Well, yeah, but here's the thing. There's a video."

* * *

The video Ruben showed me was black and white grainy mission footage. What I saw were slaloms of undulating

Hey You Assholes

gray blobs and a small white shape moving quickly across it. I stared at the video, waiting for the aliens, and then the video ended.

"That white shape was the alien?"

Ruben shrugged. "That's what I think anyway."

"What does the old man think?" I asked Ruben. The old man is what we called the captain.

"The old man," Ruben explained, "Blames the young lieutenant."

I wondered if that was fair, but at that moment Lieutenant Donnelly came back into the briefing room.

"Better not be *Braveheart*," he muttered to us.

"It's not," I said. Ruben and I looked at each other thinking the same thought. What an asshole.

* * *

The squadron went back to standard twelve-hour shifts and the ship's air conditioner broke and that became what everyone talked about. We couldn't see the aliens anymore, but just because we couldn't see them, didn't mean they couldn't see us. That's what Ruben said, anyway. And after a series of other trivial dramas, eventually people forgot that on our network, there was a video of something that no one could explain—a small white shape, skimming across a quilted night sky, moving in a way that defied everything we knew about how things from this planet were supposed to move.

* * *

"You're a progressive!" Master Guns shouted at me one day before his appointment with Chaps. "That's what's wrong with you!"

I was drafting a Red Cross message for Chaps. Someone's grandmother from another squadron had died and the sailor was going home. Normally you don't go home for dead grandmothers, but this sailor also had two dead parents and the Captain thought that warranted the expense of getting him to the funeral.

"I'm not anything," I told Master Guns, trying to concentrate. "I'm working."

"Ha! Got you!" he shouted. "Don't you see? There are no progressives. You're a reactionary!"

"I guess so," I said. I still didn't like Master Guns, but I was getting used to him.

"Here's something you can react to, shipmate," and he pulled a can of Fosters beer from his cargo pocket and set it right in front of the Oswald Chambers calendar. He crossed his arms and smirked at me.

How Master Guns came into possession of the contraband beer was the Navy has this tradition about how many consecutive days you spend at sea. If you've been underway for 45 days without hitting port, each sailor is rationed two cans of beer.

On the day Master Guns thunked the can of Fosters in front of me, the ship had just completed the deployment's first Beer Day. It's supposed to help morale, but it doesn't really work that way. It's not like you come back to your rack and see two beers on your pillow.

What they do is rope off a section in the hangar bay where they can control access to the two pallets of 24-ounce room temperature Fosters. The line to get in snakes throughout the ship.

I waited in the line like everyone else, but after an hour of getting nowhere, I wandered off. I went to the catwalks and leaned against the railing and stared at the ocean, thinking that if I was an alien that right now would be a good time to appear to a sailor standing alone on the catwalks.

Instead, the loudspeaker crackled behind me and I heard the Air Boss angrily shouting. At me.

"Shipmate in the black frame glasses and green jersey. Yes, you. There is an aircraft that is landing in approximately two seconds so would you kindly GET THE FUCK BACK IN THE SHIP."

I scurried back through the water-tight doors to see everyone in the beer line looking at me. I gave them a shrug and a little half smile, but I felt hot tears behind my eyes.

Two days later, Master Guns presented me with the can of Fosters.

"Chaps said you didn't get a beer. So I got this one for you. Just don't ask me how I got it," Master Guns said.

"Thanks Master Guns," I said, a little suspicious.

"Don't get used to it, shipmate."

I put the beer in my desk drawer, wondering what I owed him now.

Later that night I snuck the beer into my rack, which was in the berthing right under the arresting wire of the flight deck. I waited until a jet landed and using the gut-sinking crunching noise as a cover, I cracked the can and took a long draught. It tasted faintly of gold and I imagined molten liquid coating my body from the inside out.

A nice feeling, courtesy of Master Guns.

* * *

We eventually pulled into port after 102 consecutive days at sea. Master Guns laughed at me when I asked him if it was some kind of record.

"Jesus, you're green," he tittered.

Most harbors aren't deep enough for aircraft carriers so we'd drop anchor somewhere off the coast and contract smaller boats to go back and forth, ferrying sailors to land. You have to stand in a line to get on a ferry, then stand in line to get on a bus, and then you stand in line to take a taxi to a bar or the mall or McDonalds and by the time you look around to see if you can find the girl from the ship's store who Ruben said had too many freckles, but you think has just the right amount of freckles, it was almost time to start heading back.

The solution was to take shore leave. Or at least that's what Master Guns said.

"What you do," Master Guns explained to me the week before we were set to pull into the Kingdom of Bahrain. "What you do is you take leave. Shore leave. Run a chit, burn a few days of leave, and you don't have to stand watch, come back to the ship, or do anything you don't want to do."

I didn't like Master Guns, but this seemed like a good idea.

* * *

The day we pulled into port, Ruben and I stood in the long line to get on the ferry. Everyone looked strange in their regular clothes and I barely recognized Master Guns across the hangar bay in his golf shirt and khakis until he shouted at me. He was coming over to us.

"What's the plan, ladies?" he asked us.

"We took shore leave like you said," I told him.

"And?" Master Guns wanted details.

"We have hotel reservations. We're going to the diplomatic district." The diplomatic district was an area in

Bahrain, an otherwise dry country, with a bunch of hotels with bars where they serve alcohol.

"Looks like you'll be there in about four hours," he said, surveying the line ahead of us.

"That's okay, Master Gunnery Sergeant," Ruben said. "We're just happy to get off the boat."

Master Guns rolled his eyes at Ruben. "Yeah you're happy all right. Well, shit." He looked at us, thinking. "Well," he said again. "C'mon with me." And then he turned and started walking to the other side of the hangar bay where the VIP ferries were waiting.

I looked at Ruben and shrugged. We didn't know better. We went with him.

Master Guns shouted at the sentries who were guarding the VIP ferries. They let him and us through. The VIP ferry had a stripper pole below decks and a wet bar. We were the only passengers. Master Guns reached behind the bar and grabbed a fistful of mini bottles.

"Fuckin' A," he grinned.

I didn't like Master Guns and I didn't want to go with him, but I was trapped in the swirling tide of our destinies.

And there was nothing I could do about it.

As soon as we were on dry land, Ruben pulled out his phone to try and connect to the internet. "I want to see if my son is awake," he said excitedly.

"You have a son?" This information was revelatory to me.

"Do you have kids?" Master Guns asked me.

"No. Do you?"

"Me?" Master Guns made a face. "Me?" he repeated. "Kids are the last thing I need. Don't start with me about kids. I'm not going to show you all the best spots in Juffair if you keep talking about kids."

I looked at Ruben who was walking around with his phone outstretched, looking for a friendly signal. I walked over to him while Master Guns ducked behind a berm to pee.

"Master Guns wants to show us the town," I told him. I tried to keep my face blank. I knew Ruben would refuse to go with Master Guns because he knew it would be a terrible time. I also knew I could not refuse to go. For some reason, more than just the beer he gave me, I understood that my fate lay with Master Guns, out there in the half-vacant in-land of this desert kingdom.

"I am not going with that guy," Ruben said. I couldn't blame him. "I'm sticking to the plan. Come find us later."

I watched Ruben get on the bus and drive away. Master Guns walked up behind me and clapped a hand on my shoulder. "Fuck the bus. I know where to go." He licked his lips and I swallowed hard.

* * *

We ended up at American Alley which is a street close to the Navy installation lined with fast food restaurants. We went to the Fuddruckers.

Master Guns prepared me. "The beef tastes weird, but not in a bad way. It's just squishier."

The sun was setting. We hadn't come straight here. From the harbor, Master Guns had found us a taxi and he had given non-English language directions to our driver, who nodded without responding. We whizzed past croppings of high-rise buildings that looked both brand new and falling apart at the same time. Master Guns would pull out a mini bottle occasionally and take a quick snort, like it was an inhaler. He stared out the window without really looking. I knew he wasn't looking because we had been driving for close to an hour when Master Guns shouted for the driver to stop.

It turned out that whatever nationality Master Guns had assumed the driver was, he was not. We asked him where he was taking us and he shrugged.

"Do you understand the question?" I asked him.

"What even are you?" shouted Master Guns.

"Philippines," our driver said quietly.

"Philippines." Master Guns murmured it to himself like a curse. We sat in the taxi. I fought an impulse to get out of the car. It was like outer space. We had pulled over next to a decrepit billboard for Big Momma's House 2.

"Philippines?" Master Guns said again, softly this time. We were far from the city but there was a village nearby. From our distance to the hamlet, it looked undefined and almost primal, like each inhabitant was responsible for carving out their own burrow in the raw white stone of the earth.

"Then what are you doing here?" Master Guns asked genuinely. No one answered. It was a question each of us in the car was asking ourselves.

No one did anything for what felt like a long time. I had nearly convinced myself that I was dreaming when the driver turned to us and said, "American cheeseburger?" And we both grumbled approval.

I turned to Master Guns. "Where were we trying to go?"

Master Guns sneered at me. "It would've blown your mind."

* * *

And that was my first meal on shore leave. Our burgers the size of dinner plates, mangled and half-eaten. The sun set on us, two sad men in polo shirts at a Fuddruckers in the Middle East.

* * *

When the sun set, an even blacker mood descended on Master Guns. My only hope for salvaging the night was convincing him to find other sailors at bars that were nearby.

"I can hear music, Master Guns!" I was trying to buck him up. I did a little dance in my seat.

"Yeah, shitty music maybe." Master Guns pouted. It was uncomfortable for me to see and I resented him for the role it put me in. I decided I had paid whatever debt I owed to Master Guns and stood up from our booth at Fuddruckers.

"Where the fuck are you going?" he asked me.

"I'm not your ward. I'm going to a bar where there are girls and you are free to come with me," I instructed.

"What the fuck did you just say to me?" Master Guns was suddenly not pouting. "You want girls? Oh we'll get girls. Let's go."

And so we left the Fuddruckers, Master Guns leading the way. *Yay*, I thought to myself.

* * *

We passed block after block of glamorous hotel bars, packed with people. "This place," Master Guns explained, "This place we're going used to be my spot when I was stationed out here."

Across the street, we passed two sailors coming out of a hotel bar, laughing. One was laughing at how hard the other was laughing and the other one realized this and started laughing even harder. And then he laughed so hard he threw up. I looked at them longingly. We heard their laughter echo between the high rises and empty streets as we marched deeper into the city.

* * *

We arrived at a four-story white building lit from the inside with a dim orange glow. We walked in and I was surprised to discover a pretty normal bar that was sparsely filled, but did indeed contain some women. It was an even split of Arabs, Asians, and westerners.

We ordered beers, but as soon as they arrived, Master Guns grabbed his bottle and told me he was going to take a lap and I should hold things down at the bar. I watched him work the room, talking his pigeon Arabic to the locals. I could see why Master Guns liked this place. He was average height in this bar.

He made his way back to me with a smug look on his face. "I have saved the night, shipmate," he said triumphantly.

I finished my beer. "So what's the plan?"

"We're going," he paused and smiled. "We're going off-roading."

I stared at him. I didn't like Master Guns.

* * *

We went outside and Master Guns clicked a key fob high above his head and tried to locate the chirping vehicle parked somewhere in the side streets. He was talk-shouting non-stop.

"Rashid! My old landlord! Did I tell you about him? Great guy! His Jeep! Borrow it for the night! Like the back of my hand. Did it all the time. You gotta see it at night. It's gonna blow your mind! Fuck that bar! Fuck those hotels! We're going off-road! Hoorah!"

We found the Jeep, a beat-up, dust-covered thing, and we hopped in. Master Guns peeled out and almost clipped a building.

"Jesus Christ!" I said.

"Shut up," he told me.

We drove out of the city and when there were no more streetlights and the paved road ended, Master Guns launched the Jeep into the cool inky blue of the desert. Our bodies jounced over berms and sand ridges. Master Guns locked the brakes and we surfed down dunes. After a few minutes it became clear that he knew how to drive the Jeep and I started having a terrified kind of fun.

"Holy fuckin shit!" I screamed at him over the wind and whooshing of tires on sand.

"Holy fuckin shit!" he screamed back at me, smiling.

We whooped into the air. For one long moment that seemed to last for hours, I watched Master Guns shed earth's gravity. In the moonlight, I saw what he must have looked like as a teenage Marine at the start of his career. He was scrappy and debonair somehow, his face sand-whipped and ruddy. I wondered if we would have been friends if I had known him then.

I didn't like Master Guns, but I liked seeing him like this.

* * *

We stopped atop a ridge and the lights of downtown Juffair were so far away they looked like stars. We sat in the car silently. Master Guns produced the final two mini bottles and handed one to me. We were both still grinning like crazy. What can I say? I was swept up. I went for it.

"So," I started. "What happened?"

"You mean all the shit I'm in," Master Guns said.

"Yes, I mean all the shit you're in." I said. "Why?"

"What do you mean why?" Master Guns asked me. "Why the Xbox or why the woman in Reno?"

"I guess both."

"Well good because the answer is the same. Fuck them."

"You mean the Marine Corps?"

"No man, I mean everyone." He turned to look at the distant city lights. "My personal philosophy."

"Yeah," I said softly.

"Yeah," he repeated. "Don't—" and then stopped. He looked at me. "Don't be like me," he finished.

A white shape appeared in the distance and zigzagged across the sky. Master Guns seemed alarmed, but I knew exactly what it was.

"What the fuck is that?" he whispered.

"Oh," I said from somewhere deep inside myself. "Those are the aliens."

* * *

We rumbled back to civilization, crunching our tires on the rocky terrain. I expected Master Guns to return to being awful when we got closer to the diplomatic district, but he was subdued and even a little gracious. He asked what hotel I was staying at and told me it was a nice place and to get room service because the room service in this country would blow my mind.

He pulled into the circle drive of the hotel. "Thanks Master Guns," I said honestly.

He stared at me for a second, like he was weighing whether to say something else.

"Oh fuck you," he said and peeled out.

I walked into the lobby. Master Guns was right, it was a nice hotel. I was filthy from the desert. I was drunk off mini bottles and could feel sand in my teeth. The lights overhead were dim and there was a group of men sitting in high back chairs around a low table. They looked at me, gestured, and spoke to each other in Arabic.

"Super power," I said, pointing to the American flag on my backpack.

I followed the smell of cigarette smoke to the bar where I ordered a beer and finished it in one long drink.

A European-looking woman was ordering a cocktail a few stools down. She caught me looking at her so I went to take a drink of my beer, but it was empty and I made a big show of trying to get one more drop from the bottom of the bottle. I looked back over and she was laughing. She approached me and spoke with an accent I couldn't place. Swedish, maybe. "You are out of beer," she observed.

"It's nothing to be embarrassed about," I told her. "It happens to a lot of guys."

"That's pretty funny." She winked. "For an American." She kicked at my shoe playfully. I put my face in my hands. I had started crying.

"Hey what is wrong?" she said.

I heaved gigantic wet breaths. People turned around to look. I was causing a scene. "Do you ever get scared because we're all alone in the universe?" I blubbered.

She seemed to really consider the question. "Yes," she said. "I think I do."

Acknowledgements

This book would not exist without Todd Dakin, who helped me immeasurably at every stage of the process across five years. Versions of these stories appeared first in online journals like *Joyland*, *X-R-A-Y*, and *New World Writing*. The encouragement and support I received from folks like Phil Klay, Aaron Burch, Adrian Bonenberger, and many more cannot be overstated.

Kyle Seibel is a writer and US Navy veteran living in Santa
Barbara, CA. His short stories have been featured in *Joyland
Magazine*, *New World Writing*, and *Wigleaf*. This is his first
book. Follow him at @kylerseibel.

www.ingramcontent.com/pod-product-compliance
Lightning Source LLC
Jackson TN
JSHW020301170225
79125JS00002B/2